Annie O'Neil spent most of her childhood with her leg draped over the family rocking chair and a book in her hand. Novels, baking, and writing too much teenage angst poetry ate up most of her youth. Now Annie splits her time between corralling her husband into helping her with their cows, baking, reading, barrel racing (not really!) and spending some very happy hours at her computer, writing.

Also by Annie O'Neil

One Night, Twin Consequences
The Nightshift Before Christmas
Santiago's Convenient Fiancée
Her Hot Highland Doc
Healing the Sheikh's Heart
Her Knight Under the Mistletoe

Italian Royals miniseries

Tempted by the Bridesmaid
Claiming His Pregnant Princess

Discover more at millsandboon.co.uk.

REUNITED WITH HER PARISIAN SURGEON

ANNIE O'NEIL

MILLS & BOON

First published in Great Britain 2018
by Mills & Boon, an imprint of HarperCollins*Publishers*
1 London Bridge Street, London, SE1 9GF

Large Print edition 2018

ISBN: 978-0-263-07292-1

MIX
Paper from
responsible sources
FSC C007454

This book is produced from independently certified
FSC™ paper to ensure responsible forest management. For
more information visit www.harpercollins.co.uk/green.

Printed and bound in Great Britain
by CPI Group (UK) Ltd, Croydon, CR0 4YY

This one definitely goes out to my readers.
Without you this book literally could not
have been made. You are the ones
who built this hero and heroine…
I hope you enjoy their story.

Annie O xx

CHAPTER ONE

SCENT. SOUND. TASTE. Even the air felt different in Australia; so did the sea water he was ploughing through. But as the days had bled into weeks, then months, Raphael had come to know that travelling halfway round the world hadn't made a blind bit of difference. He was still carrying the same hollowed-out heart, weighted with an anvil's worth of guilt. Leaving Paris hadn't done a damn thing towards relieving the burden.

Volunteering had done nothing. Neither had working in conflict zones. Nor donating blood and platelets. He would have pulled his heart right out of his chest if he'd thought it would help. Working all day and all night hadn't helped. And then there was money. Heaven knew he'd tried to throw enough of *that* at the situation, only to make a bad situation worse.

Jean-Luc didn't want any of his money. Not anymore.

The truth was a simple one. Nothing could

change the fact that his best friend's daughter had died on his operating table.

He'd known he was too close to her. He'd known he shouldn't have raised so much as a scalpel when he'd seen who the patient was. The injuries she'd suffered. But there had been no one more qualified. And Jean-Luc had begged him. Begged him to save his daughter's life.

Raphael thought through each excruciatingly long minute they'd been in surgery for the millionth time.

Clamps. Suction. Closing the massive traumatic aortic rupture only to have another present itself. Clamps. More suction. Stiches. Dozens of them. Hundreds, maybe. He could see his fingers knotting each one in place. Ensuring blood flow returned to her kidneys. Her heart.

Her young body had responded incredibly well to the surgery. A miracle really, considering the massive trauma she'd suffered when the car had slammed into hers. All that had been left to do when he'd been called to the adjacent operating theatre was close her up.

No matter how many times he went through it, he stalled at the critical moment. There'd been two choices. He'd taken one path. He should've chosen the other. His one fatal error had built to that leaden silence when he'd returned to the operating theatre to see his junior lifting his hands up and away from her small, lifeless body.

They'd looked to him to call the time of death.

Raphael swam to the edge of the pool, blinking away the sea water, almost surprised to see that the sun was beginning to set. He pulled himself up and out of the pool in one fluid move, vaguely aware of how the exertion came easily now that he was trying to burn away the memories with lap after lap.

He was tired now. Exhausted, if he was being truly honest. Coming here to Sydney was his last-ditch attempt to find the man he had once been. The man buried beneath a grief he feared would haunt him until his dying day. He was driving himself to swim harder than he ever had before—churning the seaside pool into a boiling froth around him as he hit one side, dove, twisted, and then started again to see how soon he could hit the other—but his burning lungs did nothing to assuage the heaviness of his heart.

Love could.

And forgiveness could do so much more.

In fewer than twenty-four hours he'd see Maggie...

The years since he'd seen her last seemed incalculable. He remembered her vividly. A clear-eyed, open-hearted exchange student from Australia. Apart from Jean-Luc there had been no one in his life who had ever known him so well, who had seen straight through to his soul.

If, when they met again, she could see a glimmer of the man she'd known all those years ago he'd know there was a light at the end of the tunnel.

After toweling off in the disappearing rays of the sun, he tugged on a long-sleeved T-shirt and headed for the exit, already conditioned to look toward the white fence on the right, leading out of the baths towards the coastal path.

Le petit monstre de la mer.

He was still there. The cock-eared mutt that had been following him from his rented accommodation, along the coastal path to the Bronte Baths and back since he'd arrived in Sydney a week ago.

A reject from former tenants?

There were no tags, no chips. Nothing to identify him or his owners.

It shocked him that he'd cared enough to take the dog to a vet the day before.

At least it proved there was still a heart thumping away in his chest, doing more than was mechanically required.

He huffed out a mirthless laugh.

Or was it just proof that he desperately needed one soul in his life who wasn't judging him? Who still wanted his company?

He winced away the thought. That wasn't fair. After over a decade of virtually no contact, Maggie hadn't merely agreed to meet up with him tomorrow night. She'd found him a job at her paramedic station. She'd gone above and beyond the call of a long-ago friendship.

The memory of her bright green eyes softened the hard set of his jaw.

From what she'd said in her emails, the understaffed ambulance station sounded like a nonstop grind. Perhaps, at long last, *this* would be the beginning of the healing he'd been seeking, after eighteen months on the run from the pain he'd caused.

He certainly didn't trust himself on a surgical ward. Not yet, anyway. Perhaps never.

"*Allons-y*, Monster." He tipped his head towards the street and the dog quickly met his long-stride pace. "Let's see if we can find you some supper."

CHAPTER TWO

TICK-TOCK. TICK-TOCK.

Why had she brought him to a movie?

Raphael was going to think she hated him. But, no, she was just socially inept. And she wasn't quite ready for him to meet the "real" Maggie.

Maggie's phone buzzed in her backpack, adding to her mortification. She dragged the bag out from under her seat and fished around until she found it. Working in the emergency services meant checking your phone every time it beeped or buzzed, whether or not you were sitting next to your teenage crush from the most perfect year you'd ever had.

A year in Paris.

Raphael Bouchon.

Match. Made. In. Heaven.

Not that there'd been any romance. Just a one-sided crush that had come to an abrupt end when she'd boarded the plane back to Australia.

She pushed the button on her phone to read the message.

Dags, Dad needs more of those hyper-socks next time you come.

She speed-typed back.

They're compression socks, you dill.

Her expression softened. Her brothers were doing their best in the face of their father's ever-changing blood pressure. They were mechanics, not medics.

She glanced across at Raphael. *I could've been a surgeon, like you.*

An unexpected sting of tears hit her at the back of her throat so she refocused on her phone.

See you in a couple of weeks with a fresh supply. Maggie xx

She jammed the phone back into her backpack and suppressed the inevitable sigh of frustration. Moving to Sydney was more of a hassle than it was worth sometimes. But staying in Broken Hill forever? Uh-uh. *Not* an option.

She dropped her pack beneath her chair and

readjusted in her stadium-style seat, only to succeed in doing what she'd been trying to avoid all night—grazing her thigh along Raphael's.

"Desolé." Raphael put his hand where his knee had just knocked Maggie's and gave it an apologetic pat.

She stared at his hand. Long, gorgeous, surgeon's fingers. Strong. Assured. Not the type of fingers that caressed the likes of her lowly paramedic's knees.

Wait a minute.

Had it been a caress? If it had been then this whole high school reunion thing was swiftly turning into a dream come true. If not...

She glanced across at him and saw he wasn't even looking at her. His bright blue eyes were glued to the flickering screen twenty or so rows ahead of them. Fair enough, considering they were at a movie, but...

"Non, c'est—it's all right."

Maggie fumbled her way through an unnecessary response, all the while crossing her legs, tucking her toes behind her calf to weave her legs together and make herself as small as possible. If they didn't touch again, and she could somehow drill it into her pea-sized brain that

Raphael wasn't fabricating excuses to touch her, then maybe—just maybe—she'd stop feeling as if she'd just regressed back to her sixteen-year-old, in-love-with-Raphael self.

Ha! Fat chance of *that* happening.

Tall, dark and broodingly handsome, Raphael Bouchon would have to head back to France without so much as a *C'est la vie!* if she were ever going to give up the ghost of a dream that there had once been something between them to build upon.

The second she'd laid eyes on him tonight Maggie's body had been swept straight back to the giddy sensations she'd felt as a teen.

Two hours in, she was still feeling the effects. Despite the typically warm, late-summer Australian evening, all the delicate hairs on her arms were standing straight up. The hundredth wave of goose pimples was rippling along her spine, keeping time with the swoosh and wash of waves upon the shores of Botany Bay. Off in the distance, the magical lights of Sydney's famed harbor-front were glowing and twinkling, mimicking the warm sensation of fireflies dancing around her belly.

The outdoor cinema in Sydney's Botanical Gardens was the perfect atmosphere for romance. Perfect, that was, if Raphael had been showing the slightest bit of interest in her.

It would've helped if she didn't feel like a Class A fraud. Yammering on about living the high life in Sydney as they'd walked through the gardens toward the cinema instead of being honest had been a bad move. How could she tell him, after he'd achieved so much, that her "high life" entailed a pokey flat that needed an epic cleaning session, a virtually round-the-clock work schedule and quarterly trips to the Outback to tackle the piles of laundry her brothers had left undone.

Hardly the life of a glamorous city girl.

She was such a fraud!

Not to mention all of the appalling "Franglais" that had been falling out of her mouth since she and Raphael had met at the entrance to the gardens. Every single stern word she'd had with herself on the bus journey there had all but disappeared from her head. Including the reminder that this was *not* a date. Just an old friend showing another old friend around town.

Nothing. More.

The second she'd laid eyes on him…

Total implosion of all her platonic intentions.

Whether it was because thirty-year-old Raphael was even better looking than seventeen-year-old Raphael, or whether it was the fact that looking just a little...*haunted* added yet another layer of intriguing magnetism to the man, she wasn't sure. Either way, Raphael had the same powerful effect on her that he'd had the first time they'd met at her host family's home all those years ago.

Jean-Luc. A twist of guilt because she hadn't kept in touch with him either cinched her heart.

She'd had a lot on her plate when she'd come home. She wasn't Super Girl. She couldn't do everything.

She readjusted in her seat and gave herself a little shake. *Just watch the movie and act normal!*

About three seconds passed before she unwove her legs and twisted them the other way round. She'd seen *Casablanca* a thousand times—could quote it line for line and had planned to do so tonight, back when she'd had just the one ticket...

Maggie dropped her eyelids and attempted another sidelong glimpse at the man she'd known as a boy.

His expression was intense and focused, though the rest of the audience was chuckling at one of

Humphrey Bogart's dry comments. Smiling was not Raphael's thing.

Not anymore, anyway.

Back in Paris it had been an entirely different story. At least when they'd been together. His laugh had brightened everything, every day. It had made life appear in Technicolor.

Not that his surprise reconnection on social media had come in the form of an emotional email declaring his undying love for her—a love that demanded to be sated in the form of his flying halfway across the world to fulfil a lifelong dream of making sweet, magical love to her.

Quite the opposite, in fact.

His email had been polite. To the point. Bereft of what her father called "frilly girlie add-ons". Silly her for thinking that vital little details like why he'd decided to get in touch and move to Sydney after years of successfully pursuing an emergency medicine surgical career without so much as a *bonjour* were "facts."

Picking a movie as their first meeting hadn't exactly been a prime choice in eliciting more information either. It had just seemed a simpler way of easing back into a friendship she wasn't entirely sure existed anymore.

Back in Paris he might not have had romantic feelings for her, but there had been no doubting that their friendship had been as tight as they came.

Her eyes shifted in Raphael's direction. Seeing the sorrow, or something a lot like it, etched into his features had near enough stopped Maggie's heart from beating when they'd met up earlier that evening. Not that he was the only one who had changed…

She shivered, remembering the day she'd flown home from France as vividly as if it were yesterday. Seeing her brothers at the arrivals gate instead of her mum…their expressions as sorrowful as she had ever known them…

Leaving France had felt physically painful, but arriving home…

Arriving home had been devastating.

How could she not have known her mother was so ill?

She dug her fingernails into her palms and blew a tight breath between her lips.

It wasn't anyone's fault. It was just…life.

Her breath lodged in her throat as Raphael's gaze shifted from the massive outdoor cinema screen to Maggie's arms.

He leaned in closer, his voice soft as he asked, *"T'as froid?"*

"Cold? Me? No. This is Australia! Sydney, anyway," Maggie corrected, her nervous laugh jangling in her ears as she rubbed her hands briskly along her arms. Just about the most ridiculous way to prove she was actually quite warm enough, thank you very much.

Being in lust did that to a girl.

That, and haphazardly wading her way through a state of complete and utter mental mayhem.

Sitting next to Raphael Bouchon was like being torn in two. Half of her heart was beating with huge, oxygen-filled thumps of exhilaration, while the other half was pounding like the hoofbeats of a racehorse hell-bent on being anywhere but here.

Raphael shifted in his chair and pulled his linen jacket off the back of his seat, brushing his knee against hers as he did. Accidentally. Of course. That was the only way things like that happened to her.

Just like Raphael "deciding on a change" and moving to Australia to become a paramedic. At her local station.

Sure she'd offered to help him, completely convinced it would never actually happen. And yet here they were, thigh to thigh, sitting in the middle of the Botanical Gardens, watching a movie under another balmy summer night's sky.

Raphael held his linen jacket up to her with an *It's yours if you want it* expression on his face. He was so earnest. And kind. Not to mention knee-wobblingly gorgeous.

"Megarooni gorge", as her friend Kelly would say. Kelly would've been slipping into that jacket and climbing onto Raphael's lap in the blink of an eye. Kelly had confidence.

Maggie…? Not so much. Just the thought of climbing onto Raphael's lap reduced her insides to a jittery mass of unfulfillable expectation.

So she waved off his kind gesture, mouthing, *No, thank you*, all the while rubbing her hands together and blowing on them as she did.

Nutter. What are you doing?

"Please," Raphael whispered, and his French accent danced along the back of her neck as he shifted the silk lining of the coat over her shoulders. "I insist."

"Merci." She braved the tiniest soupçon of French as she pulled the jacket and Raphael's spicy man-scent closer round her. She mentally

thunked herself on the forehead. *Why* was she acting like such a dill?

As if the answer wasn't sitting right next to her on the open-air theater's bleacher seating, looking like a medical journal centerfold.

Raphael Bouchon, *Casablanca* and the glass of champagne he had insisted upon buying her while they were waiting for the film to start were all adding up to one thing: the most embarrassing exchange student reunion ever. Besides, it wasn't like a first date, when—

Whoa!

It's not a date. This is not a date. You are showing an obviously bereaved, gorgeous friend from high school around Sydney. That's. It. The fact that his arrival coincided with a non-refundable ticket to the Starlight Cinema and the most romantic film ever is sheer coincidence. And practical. Waste not, want not. And that includes Raphael.

At least that was what she'd keep telling herself.

Along with the reminder that this movie ended with a friendship. Nothing more.

She looked down to her fingers when she realized she was totting up the number of short-lived boyfriends who hadn't made the grade over the years. Expecting anything different when everyone had been held up to The Raphael Standard was hardly a surprise. Inaccessible. Unattainable. Dangerously desirable.

And here she was. Platonically sitting next to the man himself. Not flirting. Not reveling in the protective comfort of his jacket around her shoulders. Not trying to divine any hidden meaning behind the chivalrous gesture no one had ever shown her before. Nor was she sneaking the occasional sidelong glimpse of his full Gallic lips. The cornflower-blue eyes that defied nature. The slightly over-long chestnut hair that all but screamed for someone to run their fingers through it. Someone like her.

And yet…

The mischievous glint in his eyes that she remembered so vividly from high school hadn't shown up once tonight. And even though he'd only just turned thirty, the salt and pepper look had made significant inroads into his dark brown hair. The little crinkles beside his eyes that she might have ascribed to smiling only appeared when his eyebrows drew close together and his entire visage took on a faraway look, as if he wasn't quite sure how he'd found himself almost twenty thousand kilometers away from home.

It didn't take a mind-reader to figure out that his relocation halfway around the world was a way to put a buffer between himself and some dark memories. This was *not* a man looking for a carefree year with a Down Under lover.

Not that she would've been on his list of possible paramours. She wasn't anywhere close to Raphael's league. The fact that she was sitting next to him at all was a "bloody blinder of a miracle" as her Aussie rules footie-playing brothers would say, midway through giving her a rough-house knuckle duster.

Sigh...

Maggie feigned another quick rearrangement of her hair from one shoulder to the other, trying to divine whether Raphael was genuinely enjoying the al fresco film experience. Or *cinema en plein air*, as he had reminded her in his chocolate-rich voice as her rusty French returned in dribs and drabs. There hadn't been much call for it over the years.

She swung her eyes low and to the left. Yup. Still gorgeous.

As opposed to her.

She was a poorly coordinated, fashion-challenged dork in contrast to Raphael's effortlessly elegant appearance. Not that he'd said anything of the sort when he'd first caught sight of her at their prearranged rendezvous point. *Rendezvous?* Get her! Far from it. He'd even complimented her on her butterfly print vintage skirt and the "land girl" knotted top she'd dragged out of the back of her closet. Not because it was the prettiest outfit she owned, but because it was the only thing that was ironed apart from her row of fastidiously maintained uniforms.

Appearances weren't everything. She was proof of that. Freckle-faced redheads were every bit as competent as the next person. Well…maybe not literally, seeing as the person sitting next to her was a surgeon and she was "just" a paramedic. Anyway, her hair was more fiery auburn than carrot-orange. On a good day.

When they'd first met, in the corridors of the Parisian Lycée, she'd shaken off her small-town-girl persona and found the butterfly she'd always thought had been living in her heart. Well…a nerdy butterfly. Raphael had been every bit as nerdy as she back then. Or so she'd thought. But he'd called it…academically minded. He had been the best friend of her host's brother and she'd fallen head over heels in love with him.

Her mother had been right when she'd cheekily told her daughter to keep her eye on the "Nerd Talent." Now, at thirty years old, Raphael was little short of movie-star-gorgeous. His tall, reedy body had filled out so that he was six-foot-something of toned man magnificence. His chestnut hair looked rakishly windswept and interesting. He looked like a costume drama hero who'd just jumped off his horse after a long ride along the clifftops in search of his heroine.

Whether his cheekbones were *über*-pronounced because of the weight he claimed to have lost on his travels or because his genes were plain old superior was unclear. Either way, he was completely out-of-this-world beautiful.

Even the five o'clock shadow that she thought looked ridiculous on most other blokes added a rugged edge to a man who clearly felt at ease in the most sophisticated cities in Europe. Although she would bet her last dollar he'd do just fine in the Outback too. His body confidence spoke of a man who could change a car tire with one hand and chop wood with the other.

Not that she'd been imagining either scenario. Much.

Those blue eyes of his still had those crazy long black lashes…but shadows crossed his clear azure irises more often than not…

As if feeling the heat in her gaze, Raphael looked away from the flickering screen, giving her a quick glance and a gentle smile as she accidentally swooshed her out-of-control hair against his arm. The most outlandish hair in Oz, she called it. If she wanted it curly it went straight. Straight? It went into coils. Why she didn't just chop it all off, as her brothers regularly suggested, was beyond her.

Again she stared at the half-moons her nails had pressed into her hands. After her mum passed it had seemed as if her hair was the one thing she had left in her life that was genuinely feminine. So she'd vowed to keep it—no matter how thick and wild it became.

"So!" Raphael turned to her, with that soft, barely there smile of his that never quite made it to a full-blown grin playing upon his lips. "Did you have anything else in mind?"

Maggie threw a panicked look over her shoulder. Like holding hands underneath the starlit sky?

Gazing adoringly into one another's eyes in between soul-quenching kisses?

She glanced at the screen and to her horror realized the credits were running. Sitting beside him and not making a complete fool of herself had been hard enough, but— *Oh, crikey*. She hoped he didn't expect her to conduct an actual conversation in French. It had been hard enough when she was in her teens, but now that she hadn't spoken a word in over thirteen years…

All of her tingly, flirty feelings began to dissolve in an ever-growing pool of insecurity.

"Sheesh. Sorry, mate… Raphael. Sorry, sorry…"

She stumbled over a few more apologies. Years of being "one of the guys" at work and growing up as the tomboy kid sister in a house full of blokey blokes had rendered her more delicate turns of phrase—if she had ever had them—utterly obsolete.

She puffed up her cheeks and blew out a big breath, trying to figure out what would be best. A meat pie and a pint?

She took in a few more blinks' worth of Raphael, patiently waiting for her to get a grip, and dismissed the idea. French people didn't go out for meat pies and pints! Why had her brain chosen this exact moment to block out everything she could remember about France?

Oysters? Caviar? More champagne?

Crêpes! French people loved them. Sydneysiders did, too.

There was a mobile crêpe caravan she'd visited a couple of times when she was in between patients. She grabbed her backpack and began pawing around for her mobile to try and find out where it might be parked up tonight.

What was it called? Suzettes? Flo's Flaming Pancakes?

"Actually..." Raphael put his hand on Maggie's forearm to stop her frantic excavation. "As I am starting work tomorrow morning, perhaps we'll take a rain check?"

Maggie nodded along as he continued speaking. Something about heartfelt thanks for her help in getting him the job. The stacks of paperwork she'd breezed through on his behalf.

In truth, it was far easier to stand and smile while she let herself be swept away with the rhythm and musical cadence of each word coming out of Raphael's mouth than to actually pay

attention to what he was saying. Each word presented itself as a beautiful little stand-alone
poem—distinctly unlike the slang-heavy lingo
she'd brought with her from her small-town upbringing.

That year in Paris had been her mother's last
gift to her. A glimpse of what the rest of the world
had to offer.

She'd found out, all right. In spades.

A glimpse of Raphael's world, more like. And
she wasn't just talking about trips to a museum.

For her there was only one Raphael and he
was standing right here, speaking perfectly fluent English, his mouth caressing each vowel and
cherishing each consonant so that when his throat
collaborated with his tongue and the words hit
the ether each word was like an individually
wrapped sweet.

A *bon mot.*

She smiled to herself. Of course the French had
a phrase for it. In a country that old they had a
beautiful phrase for everything. Including the
exquisite pain of unrequited love.

La douleur exquise. And, wow, was she feeling
that right about now. Why had she been so *useful* when he'd written to her a couple of months

ago from…? Where was it? Vietnam? Or was it Mozambique? Both?

Regardless, his email hadn't suggested he was intent on coming to Australia. Just "considering a change."

Typical Maggie. She'd just picked up the reins and run with it. Filling out forms. Offering to get the right information to the right people on the right date at the right time.

"Best little helper this side of the equator," as her mother had always said.

And now that he was here…

Total. Stage. Fright.

She'd been an idiot to think—

Nothing. You're friends. Just like Ingrid Bergman and Humphrey Bogart.

"Yeah, you're right. Early to bed sounds good. In fact…" she glanced at her watch "…time's a-tickin'. Best get cracking!"

An image of Raphael tangled up in her sheets flashed across her mind's eye as the rest of her barely functioning brain played a quick game of catch-up.

"Wait a minute. Did you say you were coming to work *tomorrow*?"

"*Oui*. Didn't I tell you?" His brows cinched together in concern.

Again the nervous laughter burbled up, scratching and becoming distorted as it passed through her tight throat. "Well, yeah, I knew you were coming. My boss told us about it the other day. But I didn't—" She stopped herself.

She'd thought she'd have more time to prepare. To become more immune to the emotional ramifications of working with the one man she'd imagined having a future with. In Paris. On a surgical ward. In a marital bed. *Together.*

"Maggie, if you do not want me working at your station…"

Raphael pulled out the vowels in her name, making it sound as if she were some sort of exotic bird or a beautiful length of stretchy caramel.

Quit staring at the gorgeous man and respond, Mags.

"No. That's not it at all. I'm totally on board with it. You'll be amazing. Everyone will love you. I must've gotten muddled. It'll be nice for you. To hit the ground running, I mean."

"*Absolutement.*" Raphael nodded. "I am completely ready to be a true Australian."

Maggie couldn't help herself. She sniggered.

Then laughed. Then outright guffawed. "Raphael, I don't think you could be a 'true Australian' even if you paddled backwards on a surfboard, dropped snags down your throat and chased them up with a slab of stubbies, all with a school of sharks circling round you. You're just too…" She held her hands open in front of him, as if it was completely obvious.

"Oui?" Raphael looked straight down that Gallic nose of his, giving her a supercilious look.

Had she taken the mick a bit too hard and fast?

"What is it that I am too much of, Maggie?"

"Um…well… *French.*" She gave an apologetic shrug. "You know… You're just too French to be Australian."

The warm evening air grew thick. Whether it was an impending rainstorm or the tightening of the invisible tension that had snapped taut between them, she wasn't sure. Her body ached to step in closer. To put her hands on his chest.

"I suppose I will have to rely on you to help me," he said.

Whether he meant it or not was hard to tell.

"No wuckers, Raph," she joked, giving him a jesty poke in the ribs with her elbow, trying to defuse the tension. "I'll give you training lessons on Aussie slang and you can help me with my...um..."

Her vocabulary deserted her as her eyes met and locked with Raphael's.

"Francais?"

It would be so easy to kiss you right now.

"Maggie?"

Oh, God. She was staring. Those eyes of his...

But, again, the bright blue was shadowed with something dark.

What's happened to you since we last met?

Something about the slight tension in his shoulders told her not to push. He had his reasons for giving up his surgical career and zig-zagging around the world, only to land here in Oz. The last thing she was going to do was dig. Everyone had their "cupboard of woes," her mother had often said. And no one had the right to open them up and air them.

Just chill, Mags.

He'd spill his guts when he felt good and ready. Listening to people's "gut-spills" was one of her specialties. But when it came to spilling her own guts...there was no way she was going to unleash *that* pack of writhing serpents on anyone.

When they reached the aisle and began walking side by side the backs of their hands lightly brushed. Another rush of goose pimples shimmied up her arms, ultimately swirling and falling like a warm glitter mist in her tummy.

She was really going to have to train her body to calm the heck down if she was going to be his shoulder to cry on. Not that he looked even close to crying. Far from it.

Had she stuck her foot in it with the whole "you're too French" thing?

"For what it's worth," she said, "I really enjoy working on the ambos, and the fact you have extra language skills is great. Work is different every day. And it was an amazing way for me to get my bearings when I moved to Sydney."

"I'm not sure I'll be at the wheel. I haven't qualified for driving yet. All I know is I'm going to be working on an MIC Ambulance."

Luckily Raphael missed her wide-eyed *No! That's what I do!* response as he scanned the area, then turned towards the main bus stop outside the Botanical Gardens as if he'd been doing it every day of his life. He'd been born and bred in one of the world's most sophisticated cities— acclimatizing to another must be a piece of cake.

"I was actually surprised by how easy it was

to get my working papers. Something about a shortage of Mobile Intensive Care paramedics?"

"Yeah, that's right." Maggie nodded, her brain more at ease in work mode. "They've really been struggling over in Victoria. Well, everywhere, I think. The most skilled mobile intensive care paramedics seem to be running off to the Middle East, where the pay is better. Well, not all of them. And it's not because working here is horrible or anything… I mean it's actually pretty great, when you consider the range of services we provide to the community—and of course to the whole of New South Wales when they need it. Like when there are forest fires. Or big crashes out in the back of beyond."

She was rambling now. And in serious danger of sending Raphael packing.

He was one of the only people in her life who had known her before her mum had passed. There was something about that link that felt precious. Like a tiny priceless jewel she'd do everything in her power to protect.

Maggie looked up, her eyes widening as Raphael's expression softened into an inquisitive smile. The trees behind him were laced with fairy lights and the buzz and whoosh of the city faded into a gentle murmur as her eyes met with his.

A flash of pure, undiluted longing flooded her chest so powerfully that she had to pull in a deep breath to stave off the dizzying effect of being the sole object of those beautiful blue eyes of his. The ache twisting in her lungs tightened into a yearning for something deeper. How mad would the world have to become for him to feel the same way?

Slowly he reached out his hands and placed them on her shoulders. The heat from his fingers seared straight through her light top, sending out a spray of response along her collarbone that gathered in sensual tingles along the soft curves of her breasts. He tipped his chin to one side as he parted his lips.

Was Raphael Bouchon, man of her dreams, going to kiss her?

"I think this is where I catch my bus." Raphael pointed up to the sign above them. "I am afraid I will need my jacket back if we are going to part ways here. Will you be all right?"

"Of course!" she answered, too loudly, tugging off his jacket and checking her volume as she continued. "I'm the one who should be asking *you* that, anyway. Where was it you got a place again?"

It was the one thing she hadn't helped with. Finding him a place. He'd told her it was already sorted, but that didn't stop a case of The Guilts from settling in.

She should've offered him a bed...well, a sofa... while he sorted something out. Played tour guide. Called estate agents. Cleared the ever-accruing mess off of her countertops and made him dinner.

Not invited him to a movie and then scarpered.

But that level of support would have been slipping straight into the mode she was still trying to release herself from with her family.

The girl who did all the chores no one else wanted to do.

Besides, her home was her castle and there wasn't a chance on God's green earth that she would be inviting him round—or anyone, for that matter. She'd had almost seven years of looking after her brothers and father—enough housekeeping, laundry and "When's the tucker gunna hit the table, Daggie?" to last a lifetime.

"It's a place I found on the internet, near Bondi Beach. I thought it sounded..." he paused for effect "...Australian."

Maggie laughed good-naturedly and leant forward to punch him on the arm. At the same time he leant down to kiss her on the cheek. Their lips collided and skidded off of each other's—but not before Maggie caught the most perfect essence of what it would be like to *actually* kiss him.

Pure magic.

Raphael caught the sides of her arms with his hands, as if to steady them both, and this time when their eyes met there was something new shining straight at her. That glint. The shiny spark in Raphael's almond-shaped eyes that erased every single thought from her harried brain except for one: *I could spend the rest of my life with you.*

The fear that followed in its wake chilled her to the bone.

An hour later Maggie held a staring contest with herself in her poorly lit bathroom mirror. Red-haired, freckle-faced, and every bit as unsure whether she was a country mouse or a city mouse as she had been thirteen years ago.

Closing her eyes, she traced her fingers along her lips, trying to relive the brush of Raphael's mouth against hers. It came easily. Too easily.

Especially when she had been in love with him for almost half her life.

Her eyes flickered open and there in the mirror was the same ol' Maggie. The one who would never live in Paris. The one barely making a go of it in the big smoke. The girl born and raised and most likely to return to a town so far from Sydney it had its own time zone. In other words, she could dream all she wanted, but a future with Raphael Bouchon was never going to be a reality.

CHAPTER THREE

RAPHAEL TUGGED HIS fingers through hair that probably could have done with a bit of a trim. He chided himself for not putting in a bit more effort. For not trying to look as if he cared as much as he genuinely did.

Seeing Maggie yesterday had done what he'd hoped. It had re-awoken a part of him he'd feared had died alongside Amalie that day in the operating theatre.

When their lips had accidentally brushed last night there'd been a spark.

He was sure of it.

Enough so that he sorely regretted not kissing her all those years ago. But Jean-Luc's mother's warning had been a stark one. *"Hands off!"*, she'd said, and so he had obeyed.

If he hadn't been relying so heavily on Jean-Luc's family for that vital sense of stability his parents had been unable to provide he would've gladly risked his pride and seen if Maggie had felt the same way.

For an instant last night he'd been certain of it. This morning... Not so much.

Not that Maggie was taking a blind bit of notice of his *does-she-doesn't-she?* conundrum.

Listening to her now, reeling off the contents of the ambulance they'd be working on, was like being in the middle of an auctioneer's rapid-fire pitch.

From the moment she'd arrived at the station she'd barely been able to look him in the eye. More proof, if he needed it, that he hadn't meant to her what she'd meant to him. After all, who took someone to a movie when they hadn't seen each other in over thirteen years?

Someone with a life. Someone who'd moved on.

"Raphael?" She clapped a hand on the back door of the ambulance to gain his attention. "Are you getting this?"

He nodded, not having the heart to tell her he'd actually spent the long flight over memorizing the equipment breakdowns and layouts he'd been sent along with the confirmation of his posting.

"And over here we've got your pneumocath, advanced drugs, syringe pumps and cold intravenous fluids. It's not so much a problem this time of year. The hypothermia. What with it being summer. But…" She screwed up her face and asked, "Is hypothermia a problem in Paris?"

She quickly flicked her green eyes towards him, then whisked them back to the supply bins as if looking at him for longer than three seconds would give her a rash.

"Well, you've got snow, so I suppose so," she answered for him. Then, almost sheepishly, she turned back to him and said, "*Neige*, right?"

He nodded, parting his lips to say he was actually ready to head out if she was, but she had already turned back toward the ambulance and was reeling off yet another list of equipment specific to the MICA vehicles.

"Hey, Mags. Looks like the A-Team is being broken up."

Maggie stopped mid-flow, her green eyes brightening as a beach-blond forty-something man came round the corner of their ambulance with a timorous woman who only just prevented herself from running into him when he abruptly stopped.

"All good things must come to an end I guess,

Stevo." Maggie heaved a sigh of genuine remorse, then shot a guilty look at Raphael with an apologetic smile following in its wake.

"Raphael, this is my partner—my *former* ambo partner—Steve Laughlin."

"Crikey, Mags. It's only been ten minutes. And no lines have been drawn in the sand yet. No offence, newbie!"

He turned to the young woman behind him and gave her a solid clap on the shoulder that nearly buckled her knees before turning back to Raphael.

"Nice to meetcha, mate." Steve put his hand out for a solid shake. "You've got yourself one of Bondi Junction's finest here, so consider yourself lucky. I'm counting on you to look after her. She can be a bit of a klutz—"

"I'm more than capable of looking after myself, thank you very much!" Maggie cut in.

"Yeah, yeah. *Help me, help me!*" Steve elbowed Raphael in the ribs and laughed. "You know what I'm saying, mate? All these girls *really* want is a big strong bloke to look after 'em. Get a load of these pecs, Casey. This is what happens when your partner doesn't carry her fair share of the equipment bags."

He flexed his arm into Popeye muscles and grinned as his new charge instantly flushed with mortification.

"Yes, Steve. Nothing to do with the hours you spend at the gym instead of helping your wife with the dishes," Maggie answered drily, clearly immune to Steve's *über*-macho version of charm. "And, for the record, I think I can live *without* a big strong Tarzan swinging in to rescue me, knowing that there's a fully qualified surgeon sitting in your old seat. Twice as many patients in half the time, I'm betting."

She gave Raphael a quick *Am I right, or what?* smile.

Raphael winced. Bragging rights over his surgical skills was something he'd rather not be a party to.

"Ah, well, then." Steve gave Raphael a knowing look, completely missing his discomfort. "If you're not busy curing everyone in Sydney over the next couple of hours, perhaps you'll be able to shake a bit more fun into our girl, here. Tell her there's a bit more to life than work, will ya? When we heard you were a Frenchie we all started laying bets on how long it'd take for you to get her out on the town after her shift. She's got a thing about France, you know?"

He rocked back on his heels, crossed his arms over what looked like the beginnings of a beer belly and gave him a solid once-over.

"You're a better looking bloke than I am, so maybe you're in with a bit of a chance."

"Hardly!" The word leapt out of Maggie's throat, lancing the light-hearted tone of Steve's comments in two.

"Easy, there, Mags." Steve rolled his eyes and gave her a half-hug. "I'm just messing with you. Give the bloke a chance, all right? We're just worried about you. All work and no play…"

"Yeah. I get it, Steve. Don't you have some work you should be getting on with?"

Raphael stayed back from the group, preferring silence to watching the increasing flush heating up Maggie's cheeks.

He stepped forward for a handshake when Steve did a quick introduction of his new junior partner, Casey, before heading for their own ambulance. As soon as they'd left Maggie poured her obvious irritation into filling up all the supply bins in their ambulance.

The idea of spending time with him outside of

working hours obviously didn't appeal. Had he said something last night to offend her? Perhaps taking a rain check on a post-film drink had been bad form if it wasn't her usual *mode opératoire* to go out.

Raphael swallowed against rising frustration. Hitting the wrong note seemed to be his specialty of late. Making the wrong move. Insisting upon operating on a little girl he was far too close to, only to have to break the news to his best friend that his young daughter had just died on the operating table because of *his* mistake.

Jean-Luc would never forgive him. Not in this lifetime anyway.

He tried to crush the memory of what Jean-Luc had said to him to the recesses of his mind. A near impossible task as he revisited the cruel words each and every night while trying to fall into a restless sleep.

"You just take! All you do is *take*!"

The medical report had told a different story, had said that Amalie would have died anyway. Her injuries had been too severe. The loss of blood too great. But Raphael knew the truth. *He* was the one who had made the decision that had ultimately led to the little girl's death.

He returned his gaze to Maggie, who had shifted back into her efficient self and was doing a swirly *ta-da!* gesture with her arms in front of the ambulance.

"Clocked that? Are we good? Am I going too fast? Too slow? Should I just stop talking altogether?"

Her eyes widened and he saw that his worries about Maggie not wanting to work with him had been ridiculous. Those green cat's eyes of hers were alight with hints of hope and concern, making it abundantly clear that her nervous energy wasn't anti-Raphael. It was worry that he might not be interested. It was hope that he shared her passion for the job she loved. And, if he wasn't mistaken, there was an underlying pride at what she did for her community.

"All right, Frenchie? How're ya settlin' in, mate?"

Raphael turned at the sound of the male voice, not missing the pained expression taking hold of Maggie's face as her eyes lit on the paramedic behind him.

A tall black-haired man—big—was holding out a hand. "Marcus Harrison. Fellow paramedic. Friends call me Cyclops. I'll give you three guesses why."

Raphael threw a quick look to Maggie, who shrugged, rolling her eyes rolling as if to say, *Indulge him. It'll be over in a minute.*

When he turned back he was face to face with an eyeball.

"It's glass. Get it? I've only got one eye. Been that way since I was a nipper. Too much rugby, and one day…" Marcus pinched his fingers in front of his eye then made a flying object gesture.

Behind him Raphael could hear Maggie muttering something about *putting it away, already.*

Totally unfazed by Maggie's disgust, Marcus popped his eye back into the empty socket and doubled up in a fit of self-induced laughter. "Oh, mate. You should see your face. Priceless."

"Are you finished?" Maggie asked, her tone crisp, but not without affection.

"Yeah, but…" Marcus bent in half again, another hit of hilarity shaking him from head to toe.

"Marcus, I'm *trying* to show our new colleague the truck."

"What? He'll be all right." Marcus waved off her concerns. "You were a surgeon or something back there in Paris, right?"

Raphael nodded, knowing that a flinch had accompanied the reminder.

"Leave the poor man alone. He's got enough on his plate without you showing off your wares and quizzing him about his credentials."

Marcus strutted in a circle in front of Maggie. "Darlin', let me assure you, you can look at my wares *any* day of the week."

Again Maggie rolled her eyes. This clearly wasn't Marcus's first flirt session. Nor Maggie's first refusal. Clearly having three older brothers had toughened her up.

Marcus crossed to her, leaned in, gave her a loud smack of a kiss on the cheek, then gave Raphael a good-natured thump on the back as he passed, heading towards the tea room whistling a pop tune.

"He seems…"

Raphael searched for a good word, but Maggie beat him to it.

"A right idiot. Except—" she held up her index finger "—when it comes to work. He is a first-class paramedic. Claims he always wanted to be a paratrooper, but the eye thing made that dream die real quick—so he became another kind of para. Paramedic," she added, in case he hadn't caught the shortened term. Something the Australians seemed to do a lot of.

"And you two are…?" Raphael moved a finger between Maggie and the space Marcus had just occupied. "Were you a couple?"

He caught himself holding his breath as he waited for an answer. Was he hoping she would say no?

"Pah!" Maggie barked, her eyes almost tearing up as she laughed at the suggestion. "You have *got* to be kidding me!"

Just as quickly she recovered, throwing an anxious look towards the tea room.

"I mean, he's a lovely bloke, and will definitely make someone incredibly happy, but he's not…" Her eyes flicked to his so quickly there was no time to catch her expression. "He's a really good bloke. I'm lucky to know him. He's taught me loads."

Loyalty.

That was the warmth he heard in her voice. And it was a reminder of why he'd come to Sydney. She was loyal. She hadn't even questioned why he was here. Just helped in every way she could.

He swallowed. She didn't know the whole story.

He turned at the sound of Maggie snapping her fingers together before displaying a clear plastic bag of kit as if she were a game show hostess.

"Right. Back to work. So, we call these nifty little numbers the Advanced Airway Management Sets—or AAMS if you're in a hurry."

"*Très bien*. It all looks very familiar." He nodded, aware that his attention was divided.

Again and again his eyes were drawn to the fabric of Maggie's dark blue overalls tightening against her curves as she leant into the truck to replace the kit and then, by turns, pointed out the defibrillator, the suction kit, the spinal collars, spine board, inflatable splints, drugs, sphygmomanometers, pulse oximeters and on and on.

In her regulation jumpsuit she looked like an action heroine who donned a form-fitting uniform before bravely—and successfully—battling intergalactic creatures for the greater good of the universe.

Her fiery hair had been pulled into submission with a thick fishtail plait. Her green eyes shone brightly against surprisingly creamy skin. Ample use of sunblock, he supposed. An essential in Sydney's virtually non-stop "holiday" weather.

Instantly his thoughts blackened. As if he'd

come here for some R&R after a year and a half of trying to put some good back into the world.

"All you do is take."

There was no coming back from the death of a man's only child.

He scrubbed his hand along his neck, still hearing the heavy church bells ringing out their somber tones on the day they had laid Amalie to rest. Amalie's funeral was the last time he'd seen Jean-Luc and the rest of the Couttards.

It was the first time they had fought. The last time they had had any contact.

"You took from my parents and now you've taken my daughter. No more!"

He opened his eyes to see Maggie waving a hand in front of his face. "Hello? All right in there? Time to jump in. We've been called out. Twenty-five-year-old mother, imminent birth. We're about seven minutes out. Wheels up, mate!"

Five minutes into the ride, Maggie's internal conversation was still running on a loop.

Mate?

What was it with her and calling Raphael *mate*?

Almost as bad as Cyclops and Stevo calling him
Frenchie.

Grr... Instead of bringing out that Parisian butterfly she knew lay dormant somewhere within
her, Raphael's appearance was turbo-charging
the country girl she'd tried to leave behind in
Broken Hill.

Then again, maybe he didn't care what she did
one way or the other. It was difficult to gauge
exactly what was behind that near-neutral expression of his. Chances were pretty high that
he hadn't stayed up half the night reliving their
near-miss kiss. How mortifying. She hoped her
feelings weren't as transparent as she feared.

Pretending to check for oncoming traffic, she
gave Raphael a quick glance.

Still gorgeous. Still impossible to read.

But it went deeper than that. He didn't seem
present. And that was something he had always
been—*here,* engaged.

Could a person change so much that they lost
the essence of who they were?

She swallowed the lump of contrition rising in
her throat. *She* had. She'd changed a lot since her
bright-eyed and bushy-tailed days.

She glanced across again, unsurprised to find

his expression stoically unchanged. Not that she could see his eyes beneath the aviator glasses he'd slipped on once they'd strapped in for the blue lights ride.

"You sure you're all right?" She moved her elbow as if to prod him. The gesture was pointless as she was strapped into her seatbelt.

A curt nod was her response.

"This isn't the first run you've had since you left France, is it?"

"No." His gaze remained steadfastly glued on the road ahead of them.

Okay. Guess we're not feeling very chatty today.

Not fair, Maggie. The man's got a lot on his plate today. New country. New language. New job. Old friend...

An old friend she was having to get to know all over again.

The old Raphael would've been laughing and joking right this very second—teasing her about her driving, or about the fact that she couldn't help making her own sound effect along with the sirens and each switch she flicked. He'd maybe even have started quizzing her about why her career had gone to the blue lights instead of the blue robes of the surgical ward.

Not a freaking peep.

When she'd told him to jump into the ambulance they'd done one of those comedic dances, with one person trying to get past the other, that had ended up looking like really bad country jigging. It should have, at the very least, elicited a smile.

Not from Raphael.

Not a whisper as to what was going on with him. Why he was here. Why he had downgraded himself.

The only thing she could guess was that the man was trying to put as much space as he could between himself and some intensely painful memories.

"You know, if you want to talk or anything…"

He glanced across, his brows tugged together. "About the job? No, no. I'm fine."

"Or about other things…" She pulled the ambulance around a tight corner, grimly satisfied to see his expression change from neutral to impressed, if only for a nanosecond.

Why wouldn't he talk to her? They'd once told each other *everything*.

Everything except the fact that she was a born and bred country girl doing her best to believe it wasn't above her station to dream of life as a surgeon in Paris.

Come to think of it, neither of them had talked about their home lives much. Just the futures they'd imagined for themselves. Her host family's beautiful Parisian home had been the base for most of their adventures. And the rest of their time had been spent exploring. With a whole lot of studying on thick picnic rugs in the shadow of the Eiffel Tower thrown in for good measure. After they'd hit the books they would roll over onto their backs, gaze up at the huge steel structure and talk about their dreams for the future.

Raphael had achieved his goals in spades. Resident surgeon in a busy Parisian A&E department. Addressing conferences around the world on emergency medicine. But then there had been an the about-face, eighteen months ago, and he had gone to work in refugee camps and free clinics in developing countries only to turn up now in Sydney.

Mysteries aside, Raphael's life was a far cry from being a jobbing paramedic in one of Sydney's beach neighborhoods with no chance of climbing up the ladder.

Cut yourself some slack.

She had returned from France only to be told her mother had died while she was flying home. A girl didn't recover from that sort of loss quickly. And then there were the add-on factors: the shock of discovering her mother had known she was ill when she'd handed Maggie the ticket to Paris, the expectation of her grieving father and brothers that Maggie would step into the role her mother had filled—the role her mother had made her promise she would never, ever take.

Cramming her dream of moving back to France and becoming a surgeon into the back of a cupboard, she had cooked and cleaned and washed an endless stream of socks for her family while they got on with the business of living their lives...

It had taken her years to break out of that role. And she had finally done it. She was living life on her own terms. Sort of. Not really... Four weeks of her year were still dedicated to sock-washing, floor-scrubbing and casserole-making, but it was a step. Who knew? Maybe one day she would be the world's first ninety-year-old junior surgeon.

She glanced across at Raphael, saw his jaw

tight again as they wove their way through the morning traffic. It wasn't her driving that drew his muscles taut against his lean features. There was something raw in his behavior.

If it was ghosts he was trying to outrun, he looked as though he'd lost the battle. It was as if they had taken up residence without notice, casting shadows over his blue eyes.

If only she could help bring out the bright light she knew could shine from those eyes of his.

A little voice in her head told her she'd never succeed. *You don't have the power to make anyone happy. That can only happen from within.*

"So…" Her voice echoed in the silent ambulance as she tried to launch into the work banter she and Steve had always engaged in. "When's the last time you delivered a baby outside a hospital?"

"Is there not a midwife attending?"

Raphael's tone didn't carry alarm, just curiosity. As if he were performing a mental checklist.

"There's been a call made, but it's usually luck of the draw as to who gets there first. We'd be fighting rush-hour traffic to get to the Women's Hospital, so I don't think we'll have time to load her up and take her there. They said the birth was imminent when they rang. That the mum is already wanting to bear down."

Raphael nodded, processing.

She doubted it was the actual delivery of a child that was cinching his brows together.

Maybe…

No guessing. You do not get to guess what has been going on in his life. He will tell you when he is good and ready.

She shot him another quick look, relieved to see that the crease had disappeared from his forehead.

Work would get him on track. It was what pulled *her* out of the dumps whenever she was down. It was what had finally pushed her up and out of Broken Hill.

That twelve-hour drive to Sydney had felt epically long. Mostly because she had known she'd never wanted to go back and that it would be the first of many round trips. They weren't as frequent now…

Instead of saying anything in response, Raphael looked out of the window as they whipped past apartment block after apartment block on their way to the Christian housing charity that had put in the call.

Unable to bear the silence, she tried again. "The mother is Congolese, I think. Democratic Republic of Congo. A recent refugee. My Lingala's pretty shoddy. How's yours?"

The hint of a smile bloomed, then faded on his lips.

"Was there any more information about the mother? Medically?" he qualified.

"Nope." Maggie deftly pulled the ambulance over to the roadside. "We'll just have to ask her ourselves."

A few moments later the pair of them, a gurney, and the two birthing kits Maggie had thrown on top were skidding to a halt in front of a group of men standing outside a door in the housing facility's central courtyard.

"She's in here." One of the lay sisters gestured to an open door beyond the wall of men.

Like the Red Sea in the biblical tale, the men parted at the sight of Maggie and Raphael, letting them pass through, a respectful, somber air replacing the feverish buzz of what had no doubt been a *will-they-won't-they-make-it?* discussion.

Abandoning the gurney out in the courtyard, Maggie grabbed the birthing kits, but stepped to the side so that Raphael could enter the room first. The distant mood she had sensed in him had entirely evaporated.

Inside, curtains drawn, a crowd of women in long skirts and brightly patterned tops shifted so they could see the beautiful woman on a bed that had either been pulled into the sitting room for the birth or was there because of constant over-crowding. Either way, the woman's intense groans and her expression showed she was more than ready to push.

She was pushing.

"I'll do the hygiene drapes if you're all right to begin the examination," Maggie told Raphael.

"Good. *Bien*."

Out of the corner of her eye she watched as he unzipped one of the kit bags, quickly finding the necessary items to wash and sterilize his hands and arms in the small, adjacent kitchen, re-entering as he snapped on a pair of examination gloves. His movements were quick. Efficient. They spoke of a man who was in his element despite the dimly lit apartment and the crowd of onlookers.

But there didn't seem to be any warmth emanating from him. And that surprised her. It wasn't as though he was being mean, but… *C'mon! The woman's about to have a baby.* A little bedside manner would be a good thing to use around now!

The women, as if by mutual consent, all pressed back against the wall, necks craning as Raphael made his way to the expectant mother's side.

"You are happy with an audience?" Raphael asked the woman in his accented English, and the first proper smile to hit his lips all morning made a welcome appearance.

Finally! So it *is* there. Just hard to tap into.

The expectant mother nodded. *"Bien sûr. Voici ma famille."* She groaned through another contraction.

"Ah!" Raphael gently parted her legs and lifted the paper blanket Maggie had put in place across the woman's lap. *"Vous parlez Français? Très bien."* He turned to Maggie. "You are all right to translate on your own?"

Maggie grinned. Trust Raphael to have his first patient in Oz be a fluent French-speaker.

A seamless flow of information zigzagged from the mother to Raphael to Maggie and back again—including the woman's name, which was Divine.

Maggie smiled when she heard that. What a great name! As if the woman's mother had pre-destined her daughter to be beautiful and femi-nine. Maggie was all right as far as names went, but Daggie—as her own family insisted on call-ing her—made her feel about as pretty as if she were called Manky Sea Sponge.

"Can you believe it?" Raphael was looking up at her, his brow furrowed in that all-work-no-play look she was still trying to get used to.

"Divine? Yeah." She offered the mother another smile. "It's a beautiful name."

"This is Divine's fourth pregnancy."

Ah. That was the vital bit of information he had actually been alluding to. She'd heard. Reg-istered. Moved back to the pretty name. Was he going to be like this all the time?

Three pregnancies without any problems meant this one would likely be a cinch.

Maggie shifted her features into a face she hoped said, *Wow! Impressive!* Not, *Four chil-dren before you've turned thirty? No, thank you.*

Her mother had been down that path, and look at all the good it had done her. A life of cook-ing and cleaning in the Outback before being hit by an A-Grade cancer cluster bomb. Pancreatic.

Lymph. Stomach. At least it had been swift—though that hadn't made it any less of a shock.

"First time for a home birth?" Maggie asked, to stop herself from exploring any further her instinctual response to a life of full-time parenting. She'd been down that dark alley plenty of times, and this was definitely not the time or place for a return journey.

"*Non...*" Divine bore down, her breath coming in practiced huffs. "I have never had one of my children in hospital."

"Just as well," said Raphael neutrally, in French, "because you are crowning. I can see your baby's head now."

Cheers erupted from the women around, and to Maggie's complete surprise a chorus of joyous singing began.

Raphael indicated that Maggie should kneel down beside him as he kept pressure on the woman's perineum to prevent any uncontrolled movements while first the forehead and then the chin and finally the child's entire head became visible.

Finding herself caught up in the party-like atmosphere, Maggie beamed up at Divine, congratulating her on her ability to get through the intense moment without any tears or painkillers, and out of the corner of her eye watched Raphael check for the umbilical cord and its location.

"Are you up for one more big push?" Raphael asked over the ever-increasing roar of song. "We just need to get those shoulders out." His voice was gentle, but it conveyed how strong the determined push Divine gave would have to be.

Divine tipped her head back, then threw it forward, her voice joining in extraordinary harmony with the women around her as she bellowed and sang her way through a super-powered push.

Raphael held the baby's head in one hand, turning it towards the mother's thigh, and gently pressed down with the other to encourage the top shoulder to be delivered as Divine bore down for the one final push that…oh, yes…yes…would bring her new son into the world.

"*Felicitations*, Divine. You have a beautiful little boy."

Maggie was shocked to hear Raphael's strangely vacant tone. Why wasn't he as lifted and carried away by the raucous atmosphere as she was? No matter how often she tried to be blasé about moments like these—it was impossible. And to play a role in this miracle of a child coming into the world surrounded by song…

She might not want one herself just yet, but it was just so…so *happy*. One of those truly magical moments a paramedic could have. It brought a tear to her eye every single time.

She swiped away her tears as swiftly, expertly, Raphael suctioned the baby's mouth and nose, giving Maggie a satisfied nod to tell her that the amniotic fluid was a healthy color. Maggie handed him a fresh towel to vigorously and thoroughly dry the baby, then waited with another dry towel to swaddle the infant before gently placing him on his mother's chest.

The cooing and murmurs of delight that followed wafted and floated around them, and Raphael delivered the placenta at the very moment the midwife opened the door with a cry of, "G'day ladies, I'm finally here—no thanks to the traffic. Shall we get to it?"

Laughter, cheers and yet more singing broke out as the midwife's expression changed to one of delighted wonder when the little boy took his first proper wail.

A few more minutes of cleaning up took place while the rest of the women began handing round plates of food.

Raphael and Maggie turned to go, but stopped

upon hearing Divine calling for them. Raphael went over to the side of the bed where the little boy was, and after a bit of insistence finally accepted the child into his arms.

Again those shadows shifted and darkened his eyes. It heartened Maggie to see that the shadows weren't so dark as to mask his genuine pleasure at seeing the child was healthy and well, but there was *something* there. Something that colored even the happiest of experiences.

"What is your name?" the woman asked in her heavily accented English. "I am so grateful for your help. For my son, I must know your name."

Maggie shot him a quick look. It wasn't unknown for people to name their children after a person who had helped them in a significant way. She couldn't contain a grin. Barely twenty-four hours into his new life and already he'd brought a child into the world who might bear his name. What a way to make an impression!

One look told her he wasn't nearly as delighted by the prospect as Maggie was.

"Raphael," he said finally.

The answer was reluctant, and his posture followed suit when Divine's eyes lit up at the sound of his name. He gave an almost imperceptible shake of his head, silently communicating that under no circumstances did he want his name to go to the child.

As clearly as Maggie had read the message, so too did the new mother. She gave Raphael's arm a grateful squeeze, then stretched her arms out to him so she could hold her son close again.

"Thank you, Raphael," she said. *"Merci."*

He nodded his acceptance for the gratitude, but remained silent.

"You were amazing. You looked like you deliver babies every day of the year," Maggie couldn't help saying, feeling a puff of pride that her friend had handled the birth with such ease.

She, too, received a silent nod of thanks.

"I think," Divine continued, her eyes brightening again, skidding from Raphael to Maggie and then across to the group of women who were with them in the room, "I will call my son…"

Everyone leaned forward to hear the name of this precious new life, born into an entirely new world, his whole life stretching out in front of him with a perfectly clean slate…

"Walter."

"Walter?" Maggie clapped her hand over her mouth.

A sea of heads nodded in unison, as if it were the perfect choice. Maggie bit down on the inside of her cheek. Hard. She glanced to the side to see Raphael nodding too, as if it were the ideal name for the tiny infant.

Maybe the name wasn't funny in France, but Maggie was straining not to break down in a full fit of giggles.

Walter!

"Shall we go?" Raphael was impatient now, shifting his run bag from hand to hand as if the incident had unbalanced him.

Maybe it was being stationary that had him so fidgety. He had that faraway look in his eyes again. The unsettled one that needed the immediacy of work to dull its jagged edges.

"Sure." Maggie picked up the other run bag full of supplies, relieved to hear her radio crackling with another call-out.

As she took down her notes she tried to shrug off the disquiet that had formed between herself and Raphael.

This was a *que sera sera* situation if ever there were one.

Whatever would be would be.

Shouldering her own run bag, she received pats

of thanks on her shoulder as she passed through the group of men outside with a grim smile, furious with herself—and Raphael, if she were being totally honest—that her joy had been so thoroughly diluted.

Moments like these were her daily gold dust! Unexpected names for children. A singing birth support group. Plates full of exotic sweets being passed around as if it were Christmas Day itself. What other job gave a person access to the most intimate, personal moments in someone else's life? Sure, the bulk of them were horrible—but some, like this one, were pure sunshine.

From the look of his glowering expression, Raphael didn't really seem to "do" sunshine moments. He'd moved to the wrong country, if that was the case. Aussies were optimists. And she'd thought he was one as well.

There had been countless times when they had rolled around on the green grass at the base of the Eiffel Tower in absolute stitches. Imitating a teacher. Trying to outwit each other. Wondering what Jean-Luc was getting up to with his latest girlfriend. Or Raphael finding it hilariously funny that her favorite place in Paris was so clichéd.

She'd insisted it wasn't clichéd—it was essential. She hadn't come to Paris to hang out in burger joints or milk bars, like she could at home. She wanted all her memories to resemble the pages of the tour books she'd read before coming over.

Perhaps this—Raphael's new curmudgeonly persona—was evidence that she was the butt of another one of life's cruel jokes. The man of her dreams had come back into her life, only to be dangled in front of her like a carrot she could never catch. A carrot she wasn't entirely sure she *wanted* to catch.

"You sure you're all right?" she finally asked as they began restocking their run bags.

He shot her a look. One demanding an explanation.

"You did a great job in there. I mean, *obviously.* It's not like you're underqualified or anything…"

"But…?" He scraped a tooth across his lower lip and held it there—as if in anticipation of drawing blood if she said the wrong thing.

"It's nothing, really." She broke eye contact to reorganize the immaculately laid out supply tubs.

"Maggie, if there's something I'm not doing properly you need to tell me. Before we get any more calls." He tapped the face of his watch as if she were holding him back from a super-important meeting. On purpose.

Maggie's lips thinned. Someone had stolen Raphael and replaced him with a robot. She was becoming more certain of that by the minute.

She turned and faced him. "Your medical skills are not in question. Surprise, surprise—you're perfect." *In more ways than one.* "It's just… I thought your bedside manner would be a bit more… I don't know… *French*."

He tipped his chin to the side. "What exactly does *that* mean?"

Nice. Warm. Kind. Compassionate. Letting a woman name her child Raphael instead of Walter.

"Just…you know…a bit more Casanova than clinician."

"He was Italian."

She turned away and rolled her eyes. This was going to be a *long* shift.

Mercifully, the radio crackled, and again she tipped her head to the side to press her ear closer to the speaker on the clipped-on unit at her shoulder.

"We've got a slip and fall about ten blocks

away, and then another call after." She picked up her pace to get to the ambulance, forcing herself not to register Raphael's implacable expression.

Whatever. She'd done her bit. Helped him get a job. Taken him out for a so-so night on the town. He was a big boy.

A grown man who looked as if he was truly hurting inside.

The radio crackled again. There was a third call for them to do a hospital transport as soon as they'd dealt with their first two calls. *Good.* No time to worry about feelings. They got in the way of everything. They reminded her of all the dreams she'd let go of in an instant.

An unexpected film of tears fogged her eyes as she opened up the back of the ambulance to put her gear in. She grabbed Raphael's bag without looking and said she'd meet him up in the cab as the sting of emotion tore at her throat. How she longed to share her hopes and dreams with someone. And not just any someone. Raphael.

But he was no longer the bright-eyed optimist she'd known back then. They each bore invisible scars from the harsh realities life had thrown at them and would have to find a new way to relate to one another.

"You ready?" she asked unnecessarily as Raphael buckled up beside her after closing his door with a solid *thunk*.

"Always," he said, his eyes intently focused on the road as she pulled out into traffic.

Are you going to be this stoically bereft of charm forever? Or just when you're with me?

"All right, then."

Maggie tried to shake her head clear of the nagging thought that there was something edgy behind his response. As if he'd missed a step somewhere along the way and it had had devastating consequences. But until she knew what was really wrong, it wasn't fair to judge.

She flicked on the blue lights and siren.

"Let's get this show on the road."

CHAPTER FOUR

Stroke. Stroke. Stroke.

Raphael's arms were a blur the instant he surfaced from his dive into the seawater pool.

She'd been fine when he'd left to attend the next surgery.

As fine as someone could be when their proximal descending aorta had been near enough sheared off the heart and stitched back on again. But he had fixed it. He'd repaired the tear.

He went through the steps of the surgery again.

Traumatic aortic rupture. The tear had been sited near the subclavian artery branch, adjacent to the aorta. Sudden deceleration saw far too many injuries of this type present themselves. Surgery worked sometimes. And that time it had. He had been sure it had.

High blood pressure in the upper body. Very low below the waist. Standard stuff. Renal failure. Internal bleeding in the abdominal cavity. The accident hadn't been kind to the little girl, but he'd gone about repairing each and every tear and shear as if his own life depended upon it.

Again the water foamed and churned around Raphael as he hit the far end of the pool, dove under, circled round, then kicked off to get to the other side, oblivious to the families playing in the sea water around him.

He'd gone through the injuries in order of importance. He'd focused on her heart first. A partial aortic tear. The possibility of a pseudoaneurysm had lurked. He'd been relieved—elated, almost—to see the outermost layer of the partially torn blood vessel was still intact. This meant her small body stood a better chance of avoiding severe blood loss.

Other thoughts had lurked in the back of his mind as he'd worked his way through the cardio-vascular surgery. The possibility of paraplegia. Renal failure if the sluggish blood pressure in her lower limbs was indicating what he thought it was. Renewed aortal tears if a moderate blood pressure wasn't maintained. The ever-present threat of anesthesia taking the child's life.

But if he hadn't called the anesthetist and begun surgery she would have died within minutes of being brought into the hospital.

Two hours in, he'd been certain Amalie's cardiac functions were normal. Or as normal as they could be before he began repairing the blood vessels sheared from her kidney. Stitch by meticulous stitch he had restored blood flow to her kidneys. Renal function would return to normal once she'd had a chance to recover. It would be a long road, but she was a survivor.

He remembered telling himself that when the call had come for another surgery.

All that had been left to do was close her up. Something any junior doctor could be relied on to do.

He'd had to make a choice. There hadn't been any other qualified surgeons available to help. He'd simply had to make a choice.

He gasped for air when he hit the far side of the pool and then began again.

He should have known that even so much as a hint of high blood pressure would exacerbate the tears he'd so diligently stitched back together. That she would go into cardiac arrest. That the junior surgical staff wouldn't be able to massage her poor, damaged heart back to life.

All this while he had been saving a life in the

next room. *That* patient had lived. Had told him he was a hero.

Jean-Luc had called him something else. Lots of things he simply couldn't shake.

A murderer. Careless. Reckless.

Raphael knew grief made people say things they didn't really mean, but later, when he'd shown up at the funeral, Jean-Luc had known exactly what he was saying and the damage it would do to their friendship. Making it as irreparable as the injuries Amalie had been unable to survive.

"All you do is take!"

No matter how hard he pushed, how powerfully the blood roared between his ears, Raphael still couldn't drown out the memories.

Coming to Australia had been a mistake.

The Arctic, Brazil, the moon… Nowhere was far enough to outrun the burden of guilt chasing him down like a pack of savage wolves.

He'd thought seeing Maggie again would be the salve he needed. A reminder of the man he had once hoped to become.

She was trying. God knew she was trying her best to elicit a bit of good-natured fun from him as they went from patient to patient, but he just didn't seem to be able to do it. The whole idea of getting someone to the hospital and leaving their care to someone else echoed the situation with Amalie and knocked his response time out of sync. As if his timing was permanently a beat or two behind what it had once been, diminishing his ability to relate to people in real time.

In the refugee camps in Mozambique he had convinced himself it didn't matter. The mass of humanity there had been so overwhelming, their need for care so urgent, that patient had blurred into patient as the weeks had turned into months without his seeming to have noticed.

So he'd moved to Vietnam. The free clinic there—funded by a wealthy French businessman—had been built specifically to allow physicians more time to establish a doctor-patient relationship. There he'd been allowed to have the follow-through he hadn't been able to provide in the A&E. And he'd tried. Tried to make connections. Tried to open his heart.

It had been like tapping blood from a stone in the end. No dice.

He'd told himself it was the language barrier... conveniently forgetting the fact that many of his patients spoke French in some form or another.

He just didn't seem to have it in him to connect anymore.

Not with the beautiful newborn he'd held in his arms. Not with the grandmother who had slipped in the shower and seemed to have bruised her ego more than her hip. Or the drug addict who had, after refusing treatment twice, finally begged them to take him to rehab, give him a chance to start again.

Another chance. That was all *he* wanted. Another chance to prove that he was a good man beneath this ever-darkening cloak of grief he didn't seem to be able to shake. Another chance to look into Maggie's eyes and feel worthy.

He swam until his lungs burned with exertion and then pushed himself up and out of the seaside pool. Without turning back or looking down he began his long-legged stride, with the cock-eared mutt faithfully matching his pace.

What the little monster saw in him he'd never know…

Before he turned down the walkway leading to his rental cottage he stopped and stared at the dog.

"Qu'est-ce que tu veux, eh?"
What is it you want from me?

He stared at the scrubby-looking mutt. No collar. A little ribby beneath the multi-colored wire-haired coat, but not starving. Definitely not a pure breed. A slightly crooked gait, as if he might have had a broken leg at some point, or endured some form of trauma he'd never properly healed from. He would carry traces of that injury forever.

Raphael knew the feeling.

"Life's not fair—is it, *mon petit monstre*?"

The dog shook his head at him, maintaining eye contact the entire time.

The corners of Raphael's mouth tugged downwards in one of those rueful smiles he'd used to see his father give when Raphael had presented him with his latest set of exam results.

"Eh, ça va," his father would say, disguising any pride he might have felt with chastisement. "You'll do better next time, won't you, boy?"

His mother had never looked once—too busy "catching up" with her friends over yet another bottle of red wine.

And his marks had always been perfect.

Raphael opened the low wooden gate and let the dog into the small garden. Everyone deserved a break.

Leaving the dog outside, he went into the kitchen and pulled a takeaway container out of the refrigerator—some grilled chicken he'd bought a couple of days earlier but never got around to finishing.

Back outside on the small veranda he unceremoniously sat down on the steps leading into the garden, where the little monster waited with a patient expression on his little furry face.

"Asseyez-toi. Ici," he said gruffly, handing the dog a piece of chicken once he'd obeyed the command to sit beside him.

A few moments passed in companionable silence until he felt as if something had begun to thaw within him. Perhaps one day Jean-Luc would see he had done the best he could. Would know a surgeon's life was full of critical choices and that at the time... *No.* He'd had to make a choice and he'd made the wrong one. *He* was the one who would have to own the mistake. Jean-Luc had enough to bear without adding forgiveness to the mix.

Raphael reached out and gave the dog's head a rub. *"Alors, mon ami.* How about I teach you some French?"

CHAPTER FIVE

MAGGIE HELD THE mobile phone at arm's length and stared at it in disbelief. Had her brothers gone completely mental? Why would she want to drive twelve hours to make a birthday cake... for *herself*? The least they could do was crack a couple of eggs into a bowl and throw in some sugar and flour.

"Aw, c'mon Daggie," her older brother cajoled.

Maggie flinched at the childhood nickname and took a deep breath as he continued.

"You know Daddo would love it. He hasn't had your choccy cake in I don't know how long."

Maggie did. About five years, eleven months and a handful of days ago. The day she'd turned twenty-four, called enough enough and packed her meagre stash of belongings into the rusted-out ute her brothers had refused to drive.

She'd upgraded her car in the years since, but she wasn't so sure how much progress she'd made on achieving her dreams.

"I'll think about it."

"Dad's not getting any younger, Mags," her brother said, his voice completely sober this time.

"I know. I didn't say I wasn't coming, I just said I couldn't believe you're putting in recipe requests."

Maggie swallowed away a thousand other things she could have said. Facts she could throw back at him. Like the simple reality that Sydney didn't exactly have a fortress wall around it, forbidding them from visiting *her*. They had cars. The ability to book a train. There were flights. Daily.

Who said *she* was the one who always had to rearrange her life to accommodate them? To go back to a place that held so many bad memories?

Her mother's voice rang in her ears, clear as a bell. *"They love Broken Hill, Maggie-moo. Let them. You're my little wandering star. Now, go shine and make the world a brighter place."*

The ache that never seemed to have lessened since her mother had passed tightened in Maggie's chest as her brother continued his campaign for her to make sure she included her birthday in her next trip. There'd be a barbie. And a bonus:

the washing machine was broken so she wouldn't even have to worry about catching up on laundry.

Out of the corner of her eye she saw her old ambo partner Steve approach the bulletin board she'd parked herself in front of but had yet to examine.

"I gotta go, Nate. Work."

Her eyes darted across to the new staff rota. Maybe now Raphael had had a bit of acclimatizing he'd be all right with another partner.

"You better mean it, Dags. The thinking about it," Nate said, his voice carrying a bit more warning than it usually did when he made his "time to come home" calls.

"Yeah."

She clicked on the red handset symbol on her phone and felt the weight in her chest sink to her gut. No matter how many times she'd been home since she'd moved to Sydney fear still built in her chest as strongly as it had when she'd boarded the plane at Charles de Gaulle airport.

She'd buckled into her seat thinking she would have time. Time to tell her mum how much she loved her. How she had, at last, found her place in the world.

She'd disembarked to be told she had to find herself a black dress for her mother's funeral.

She'd been three hours late.

One hundred and eighty minutes short of telling her mother she loved her.

"Looks like you and I are busted up forever, Mags."

"What do you mean?" Maggie followed the line Steve was drawing along his neck before he flicked his thumb toward the new staff rota.

"No more you-and-me squad, from the looks of things. Tough luck. For Casey, at least. You've got yourself a cracking good partner. Not as good as me, of course…" Steve shrugged, shaking his head along with her as she finally connected the dots.

Maggie and Raphael were to be permanent partners.

She stared at the roster in horror. She hadn't protested—much—when she and Raphael had been posted together for the first couple of rounds of shifts, but now it seemed the chief wanted him to be her permanent partner.

Her boss was plain cruel. Hadn't he *seen* how hard she was finding it, working with a man who seemed to elicit every emotion she'd ever hidden from? Lust. Hurt. Complete and total unrequited love.

To name but a few.

Was she still attracted to him?

More than ever.

Was he an incredible doctor?

Hands down the best she'd ever worked with.

Did she want to be stuck in an ambulance with him for the rest of her working days, only for him to discover she hadn't even come close to applying for medical school, let alone got in?

Not a chance in hell.

Whenever Raphael looked at her she felt as if she was being X-rayed. As if he was trying to figure out what had changed. What was different.

She could answer that easily enough. She wasn't the person she'd let him believe she was when they'd been in Paris. And when she'd come home her whole world had changed.

For that one blissful year she hadn't mentioned her Outback upbringing. Not once. She hadn't exactly lied. There had been no fictional sophisticated past she'd had to scramble to remember. But she hadn't exactly been forthcoming about the way she'd really been raised.

Not that she was embarrassed about it. She

loved her family. Even if they *were* a bunch of lunkheads. It was just… They were so…*content*. And she'd always dreamed of life being so much *more*. Sometimes she envied how plain old-fashioned happy they were.

Pffft. Well. Stuck in an ambulance together for pretty much three entire days at a time, Raphael was bound to figure out she was a small-town girl whose dreams hadn't really got her all that far.

Already her cheeks burnt with embarrassment at what she would have to admit to.

Years ago she had dreamt of working with Raphael. Scalpel by scalpel, suture by suture, as they approached each and every surgery with the same tenacity and *joie de vivre* they'd seemed to elicit in each other. Countless hours they'd spent talking about it—discussing which classes they'd need to take to get into pre-med programs, quizzing each other on the different disciplines they'd like to study.

Hand on heart, they had even jinxed each other after simultaneously shouting out, "Trauma surgeon!"

Jinxed was right. For her, at least.

That day as they'd sat near the Eiffel Tower—at

her insistence, of course—she and Raphael had crossed their hearts and made up a silly handshake to confirm that they would each do everything in their power to work together as surgeons one day.

She'd truly believed all her dreams would come true. But when she'd returned home it was as if she'd never had them in the first place.

She'd remembered getting almost dizzy as they'd tipped their heads back and tried to see all the way up to the top of the Eiffel Tower, making a promise that in ten years' time they would come back and compare notes. Then again in twenty.

Little had he known she was hoping they'd also be seeing each other every day in between.

Little had he known how the bubble of perfection she'd woven into her heart had shattered into a thousand irreparable pieces when she'd flown home the following day.

She watched now as her old partner made his way to his ambo, prepping it for the day's jobs.

She sternly reminded herself that being a paramedic *wasn't* second best. She loved it. Much more than she'd anticipated. It was a way of reaching people who often had no one else in their lives. She'd seen it countless times—particularly with the elderly. She loved knowing how a simple chat, a moment of human connection, was often all they were after. And she was more than happy to be the person to bring a smile to their face.

Besides, she was good at it. The human touch part. After she'd finally moved to Sydney she'd considered going to pre-med night classes, but life had got busy and she was always knackered at the end of her intense shifts.

At the end of the day, *she'd* given up on her hopes and dreams and Raphael hadn't.

He was the most driven person she had ever met. Lycée. Pre-Med. Med School. Surgical Intern. Surgical Resident. He'd hit every one of his goals as if his life had depended upon it.

There wasn't a chance in the universe he'd ever want to be with someone who had given up at the first hurdle. Even if it was the biggest hurdle she'd ever had to leap. This whole "slumming it" thing on a paramedic crew was obviously a blip on his timeline. Something he would look back on and wonder, *Why did I do that?*

"Maggie?"

The sound of Raphael's voice threw Maggie's tummy into its usual tailspin of swirls and loops.

"I'll meet you at the truck in five," she called across to him, heading to the station chief's office.

Masking how she felt about Raphael was getting harder and harder. Not only had it thrown her long-dormant feelings into full-on active volcano mode, but his brooding presence was also starting to impact her ability to treat her patients with one hundred percent focus.

That was a line she was completely unwilling to cross. And she wouldn't leave her boss's office until he understood her, loud and clear.

"Everything all right?" Maggie smiled across at Raphael as she clicked open her door, but the note of anxiety in her tone was echoed in her green eyes.

He nodded. He was the one who should really be asking *her* how she was doing. As if he didn't already know.

She jumped out of the ambulance and closed the door with a solid clunk.

"I think he hates me."

The words were still ringing in his ears nine hours into their shift. He'd overheard Maggie speaking to the station chief before they'd started work this morning. This was their third round of three days on, four off, and it looked as if she'd had enough of him. Perhaps coming to her favorite food truck was her way of letting him down gently. Sugaring the pill before letting him know that things simply weren't working out.

He hung his head and gave the back of his neck a rough scrub. This wasn't right. Just letting things fall apart. He had tried to make things right with Jean-Luc but it had been too soon. Too fresh. He saw that now. But he had the ability to change the here and now.

"Stay with my little girl."

He shrugged his shoulders up and down, then climbed out of the ambulance. He had to rid himself of the toxic emotions that had been feeding on each other, multiplying instead of diminishing. It was an unhealthy pattern and it needed to be broken.

The thought of losing Maggie was the spur he needed. He knew he wasn't a barrel of laughs to work with, but *hate*? He didn't *hate* her.

He admired her.

More than that.

He lifted his eyes up to the heavens for inspiration.

He was *grateful* to her. Grateful to this woman

who'd unquestioningly helped him when he'd written to her from Vietnam. She hadn't asked a single question. She'd simply helped. And when he'd arrived she hadn't pressed, not having the remotest clue why he had changed from the laughing, trivia-obsessed pre-med student she'd met all those years ago to this darker version of the man he'd hoped to become.

She wasn't the only one who'd stopped writing when they'd said goodbye all those years ago in Paris. But she was the one who had kept her heart open. The one he'd come to when his own heart had been worn raw with effort to atone for a mistake he could never change.

The simple truth was that Maggie Louis was the only person left on earth who treated him with respect.

A vinegary twist of guilt tightened in his gut. Not telling Maggie about his past—what he'd done that awful day at the hospital—was akin to lying to the one person who deserved his honesty more than most.

A shot of energy surged through him and gripped his heart.

He couldn't lose her. Not now.

He hadn't travelled around the world only to let

her slip through his fingers. He'd lost Jean-Luc's precious friendship. And Jean-Luc's parents'. Not that the Couttards had spelled it out for him, but he knew there was no coming back from the loss of a beloved child and grandchild.

Well, he was damned if he was going to let Maggie slip away. Not this soon. Not without letting her see the real him.

She needed to know about the Raphael who'd grown up in a wealthy neighborhood—not in a beautifully appointed home like Jean-Luc's, as he'd let her believe, but a few blocks away on an estate for low-income families. She needed to be told about the teenaged Raphael who had fallen head over heels for her but only offered friendship after Jean-Luc's family had cautioned him to keep things platonic.

Maggie deserved to understand why he'd honored the request. How Jean-Luc's family had all but raised him, virtually adopting him after his own parents had passed away the summer he'd finished Lycée. He couldn't have compromised that level of support. Support he'd known he'd need if he were ever to come good on his dream of becoming a doctor.

The near-impoverished upbringing...the less

than loving parents. They were things he'd been able to put behind him. And now he had to find a way to learn from the experience of Amalie's surgery and put that behind him, too.

Maggie needed to know he'd become the man he'd promised her he would become one day. But now he'd lost track of that man. And he'd sought out the one person he thought could help find him again.

He closed the ambulance door behind him with a renewed sense of purpose. He would tell Maggie everything. And when the slate was clean he'd live with the ramifications.

She would either accept him or say goodbye. But he would not let her believe he hated her. Or let her "dump him" over a gourmet sandwich across the street from the beach. Not until she knew the truth anyway. After that, the decision was solely hers.

Raphael rounded the ambulance to where Maggie stood, glanced across at the brightly colored food truck, then back to Maggie. "So, this is the best food in Sydney?"

Start small. Aim high. Earn this. Earn the place in her heart.

She nodded. "I think so, but I suspect your standards may be a bit higher."

"I'm always open to trying new things."

Her eyebrows shot up, then cinched together. "Well… I like it, anyway. Hopefully you will, too."

Lead. Balloon.

He was going to have to ramp up his conversation skills.

"Do you remember that last day we were in Paris?"

Her brow furrowed. Okay. It was a bit of a non sequitur, but he could see it so clearly.

"At the Eiffel Tower?"

She gave an embarrassed laugh. "I made you go there loads, didn't I? You must've thought I was a right nutter."

"Remember it was raining?"

She'd been twirling round one of the lampposts as if she was in a musical. It was the most free-spirited he'd ever seen her. There had been a fraction of a second when the ache to pull her into his arms and kiss her had been almost overwhelming, but he'd made a promise to the Couttards. That friends-only promise had been one of the hardest he'd ever had to keep.

"Yeah, well, that was a long time ago. So…" She sucked in a big breath and pasted on a smile. "Now it's all sunshine and tucker trucks! Who would've thought it, eh? From Paris to…uh… Tuckerville."

He arched a perplexed eyebrow.

"Tucker truck? Not heard of that? Food. Food is tucker. So…" She tipped her head toward the truck and gave a shy grin. *"La cuisine…c'est superb!"*

She exaggerated her French accent—a habit, he noted, that she fell back on when she was unsure of herself. The ache returned. The desire to kiss her. Hold her. Be the man she wanted to swing round lampposts and sing in front of.

He had to tell her. Tell her everything.

Together they took another step forward in the admittedly impressive queue, and after a moment she asked, "Don't you have food trucks in France?"

He nodded. More with each passing year if memory served. Food might top most French people's list of Important Things About Being Alive, but it hadn't been anywhere on *his* radar during those last six months he'd been in Paris.

Food had become merely something he had to consume in order to stay alive.

Maggie took in a big breath and popped on that nervous smile of hers again. "I probably should've brought you here the first day we worked together, but—" She stopped herself short.

He knew what she was going to say...what she *should* say. *I would've brought you here earlier if you hadn't had such an enormous thundercloud hanging over your head since you arrived.* Or, as a more straightforward Australian would've said, *If you hadn't been so bloody rude after all the hospitality and kindness I've showed you.*

"They say good things come to those who wait."

His eyes drifted to the menu hung alongside the service windows of the silver caravan. He'd have to meet those catlike green eyes of Maggie's soon. Answer her questions. Tell her the truth.

"Well, I know it's just my opinion, but Betty's Big Baps is totally worth the wait." She grinned as she said the name. Then giggled. "I just love saying the name of this place. I don't know if I love the name more, or the sandwiches."

He tried to return her smile—the first genuine one he'd seen on her all shift.

Maggie didn't miss the fact that the smile didn't make it to his eyes.

She turned away and feigned interest in a couple of surfers joining the queue. They were laughing, regaling one another with stories of the waves they'd caught. Light. Free.

The two words caught his attention. He hadn't felt either one in eighteen long months.

Driven. Determined. Committed. Those words worked.

Driven to do penance for his mistake? Determined to do—what? Go over and over a surgery he couldn't re-do until the details eventually began to blur? Committed to staying out of Jean-Luc's path to avoid any more painful confrontations?

That was a coward's way out.

And he was no coward.

As his gaze returned to Maggie he was suddenly struck by the delicacy of her features. The smattering of freckles across her button nose. The gentle angles of her high cheekbones. The delicate swoop and dip at the apex of her upper lip. One that was begging to be traced with a finger. With a tongue. She was a beautiful woman. And he hated it that he was the reason behind the uncertainty in her gaze when their eyes finally met.

It's not brain surgery. Start a conversation.

He nodded at the ten or so people in front of them. "What if we get a call?"

Nice one. Très bien. *You really have mastered the art of embarking on a meaningful* tête-à-tête, *Raphael.*

"No worries on that front," she replied. "The station chief has promised us half an hour off before sending any more calls our way since we've been flat out all day. It's worth the wait. Honest. You won't have tasted anything like it before. *C'est magnifique!*"

A soft smile softened the usual hard set of his mouth. Maggie had been dappling her conversation with French with increasing frequency, but she was still twisting her forays into his native tongue into a comedic parody. As if she didn't quite trust herself to just...*speak.* She'd been practically fluent when she'd left. Had all the confidence she'd gained over the course of her year in France disappeared?

The thought detonated another black hole in his chest.

He knew how easily confidence could take a knock.

When he'd walked out of that surgical room he'd been one hundred percent certain Amalie would make a full recovery. He had told himself that hanging around just to make sure was an instinct he wouldn't have had if she'd been a stranger. Walking away was what he would've done with any other patient.

But ten minutes later it was as if he'd entered a different time and space continuum. He should have stayed. The instinct hadn't been a case of emotional involvement. It had been a surgeon's decision—and he'd gone against it.

His team of junior surgeons had tried their best to resuscitate her. He'd come as soon as he'd heard the Code Blue had been called. And it had still been too late.

As a group, the surgical team had looked up to the digital clock and they'd all waited for him to call the time of death. Then they had each followed suit, as per protocol. The same protocol that had dictated he had been too close to the patient to be her surgeon.

Hearing the collective confirmation that Jean-Luc's only daughter had in fact died in his care had been akin to receiving an axe-blow to his heart.

A part of him had died that day too. And the quest to find it again—that vital spark that had made him courageous enough to believe he could perform surgery on the most critically injured people and give them another shot at life—had brought him here. To Maggie.

A gentle sniggering at his side brought him back to the present.

"I still can't believe you let that poor child start going through life being called Walter." Maggie was shaking her head in disbelief.

"Sorry?"

"The baby from our first call-out? The other week?" Maggie prompted. "He was adorable. Absolutely gorgeous, with chubby little cheeks and a little round belly. He would've been even more adorable if he'd had your name. *Walter?* You really think he's going to be down with the kids with a name like that?"

"Raphael isn't exactly a guarantee of a gilded life."

Maggie sucked in a sharp breath, rolled her eyes to the cloudless sky then swore softly under her breath. Not something he'd ever heard her do.

"*Desolé*. I'm sorry, Maggie." He tugged his fingers through his hair. "I seem to be hitting all the wrong notes lately."

She gave him a sharp *no kidding?* look, her features instantly melting with a wash of remorse. "Don't worry. We all have off days."

Days. Months. Years, almost.

Everyone in Paris had eventually drawn back. Not that he blamed them. Until he made things right with Jean-Luc and his family he was no good to anyone. He'd gone to their homes to try and explain, to apologize, each time knowing whatever he'd say wouldn't be enough. Could never be enough.

All you do is take!

There was truth in those words. He'd taken their love. Their hospitality. Their kindness.

Their daughter and grandchild.

Every single time he'd raised his hand to the door to knock, he'd turned and walked away.

"What'll it be, mate? Big Bap? Little Bap? Cardboard box?"

Without his having noticed, they'd reached the front of the queue.

Maggie was tipping her head toward the rotund sandwich vendor. "You're up, Raphael. I'm having the Pie-Eyed Pastrami. What'll you have? My shout."

His heart softened at the hopeful expression playing across her features. He owed her kindness. The kindness he seemed to be able to show the little mutt who still followed him faithfully from the seaside pool and back every night. But extending it to a *person*… Too risky. Too painful.

"Raphael? Your order?" Maggie gently nudged his arm.

"Yes, of course. Um…cheese. A plain cheese sandwich with be fine."

"We don't do plain old cheese, mate." The counter clerk looked at him as if he'd grown an extra head, then changed his disbelief into a suggestion. "We've got a Buttie Brie Blinder. Would that float your boat? It's got horseradish and some properly ponging brie in it. I can stick some beetroot in there for you if you like. Adds sort of a vinegar twist. A real ripper."

Raphael blinked up at the vendor, not entirely sure how to respond.

"Smelly cheese," Maggie prompted, her brows cinching together. "You know… Brie. Just like at home, in France. You always said cheese wasn't any good unless you could smell it a block away."

She laughed at a sudden memory. "That's how you taught me which cheese was which. The smell-o-meter."

He looked at her, almost confused as to who she was referring to. Had he *ever* spoken with her about cheese in such a light-hearted way?

"He'll have the Blinder," Maggie told the perplexed-looking vendor, and then, after collecting their drinks, steered Raphael over toward an empty picnic table under the shade of a large tree a few meters from the van. She handed him a cold bottle of water. "Here. You don't seem entirely with it. Probably dehydrated. You've got to remember to keep drinking water. It's really easy to dehydrate here. Even in the winter."

"You shouldn't be working with me."

The words were out before Raphael could stop them. And they had the opposite effect to what he'd been hoping for.

Maggie's body language instantly shifted from open to closed. A woman protecting what was left of her dignity in the wake of an excruciating dressing-down. She pushed aside the packet of crisps she'd bought unopened, and began toying with the lid of her water bottle.

"Um... Raphael. I've actually already spoken to the chief. You're obviously in a different league to me, so it shouldn't be too hard to get you transferred to a different station or working with a different partner. It's pretty obvious you and I aren't exactly a match—"

"Non."

Her eyes widened as he held his palms up between them.

Fix this. Now.

"No, no, Maggie—that isn't it at all."

"Look, there's no need to try and cover up the fact that things have not exactly been relaxed between us." She looked away for a moment, swallowing the emotion rising in her throat. "I know we were friends back in the day, but things change. People change."

He had to stop this before it went too far.

"Maggie, it's *me* who is not worthy to work with *you*."

"What are you talking about?" Her green eyes widened again, this time in disbelief. "You're a qualified surgeon. You've worked around the world. All I've done is my paramedic training and then managed to move from a small town to a big one."

He shook his head and lifted a hand to stop her. "Please, don't do that."

"Do what?"

"Put yourself down. You are…" He reached across the table and took Maggie's hands in his before she could withdraw them. "You are, hands down, one of the kindest, most qualified medical personnel I have ever met."

She huffed out a disbelieving laugh. One entirely bereft of humor. "If you're going for flattery to let me down easily, please don't bother. Look." She threw a look over her shoulder. "The sandwiches will be ready in a minute. We've not eaten all day, so let's just get our blood sugar back to normal, get through the rest of our shift and then I'll ask the chief again for one of us to be transferred. They need people everywhere in Sydney, and with someone of your caliber it shouldn't be a problem. Easy-peasy."

She looked as miserable as he felt. And that was when it hit him. She cared for him. And not just as a friend.

Hard-hitting waves of emotion bashed against his chest, one after the other. Disbelief. Concern. Regret. And then, like the smallest ray of sunlight penetrating a sheet of pure darkness…hope.

Hope that if Maggie could still see something good in him there might be a way for him to redeem himself.

He moved the crisps and their drinks to the side and reached across the table, tipping Maggie's chin up with a finger so that her gaze met his. The sheen of tears glazing her eyes didn't come as a surprise. But his response to them did.

He had nothing to offer Maggie right now and she needed to know why.

"I killed a child, Maggie. I don't know who I am anymore. I think I came to you so I could remember who I once was. To see if I could be that man again."

CHAPTER SIX

MAGGIE STARED AT the foil-wrapped sandwiches the vendor had deposited on their table, swiping at the tears spilling freely onto her cheeks. The ability to breathe had been snatched from her. She forced herself to meet Raphael's gaze, knowing it hadn't left her since he'd dropped his bombshell. She didn't recognize her own voice when she finally spoke.

"A child? What do you mean?"

Raphael tipped his head into his hands for a moment, and when he raised it again those dark shadows all but obliterated the blue in his eyes.

"Her name was Amalie," he began, his voice hollow with grief. "She was my best friend's daughter."

"You mean Jean-Luc?" Disbelief was icing her veins. "But... I don't understand. You would never do anything like that. *Never.*"

"She was in an automobile accident," Raphael conceded.

Maggie felt the pounding of her heart descend from her throat to her chest as he continued in that same, painfully toneless expression.

"It was a motorway pile-up. One of those multi-car incidents that happen when everyone's in a hurry and a thick fog descends. One minute everyone was driving at the national speed limit and the next—" He made a fist and rammed it into his other hand.

The gesture was so finite that Maggie flinched against the suggested screech of tires and clashing of metal on metal as one car ran into another.

"Were you in the car?"

Raphael shook his head. *"Non.* It was Jean-Luc's wife, Marianne, and their daughter Amalie who was three."

Maggie's curiosity flared. This was the first time she'd heard him mention Jean-Luc, though she'd tried raising the topic a couple of times. Pressing for details would have meant explaining that she'd dropped the ball too, so she hadn't pursued it.

She'd stayed with Jean-Luc's family for her student exchange year and they had been unbelievably kind and generous. Over the year she had wanted to write to them so many times, to tell them how grateful she was for that incredible year in Paris, but apart from the quick thank-you note she'd forced herself to write she had ceased all contact.

She should tell him. She would. But this was *his* time.

"What happened?"

"Marianne suffered superficial injuries and a couple of broken ribs, but was fine. Thank heaven. But Amalie—she suffered massive internal trauma when another vehicle hit theirs from the side."

Maggie's fingers flew to cover her mouth. "I am so sorry."

Raphael's brows cinched together as he huffed out a frustrated sigh. "Don't be. Not for me, anyway."

"What are you talking about?"

"We were all going to go for supper after Jean-Luc and I had finished work. You know he's become an amazing lawyer?"

His sad smile was in direct contrast to the pride in his voice that his friend had done so well.

"I don't see why this means I can't feel sorry for the loss you suffered. You two were so close. Amalie must've been like a—"

He shook his head. He didn't want her to say the words. *Like a daughter.*

Had he wanted children? Lost one of his own?

"Going out was my idea. We'd moved to different areas so didn't see each other socially as much. Nothing fancy. A walk along the Seine... Amalie always enjoyed watching the boats, so we had picked a little restaurant on Ile Saint Louis."

Something flickered in his eyes. Was it the same memory that had popped into Maggie's mind? Of that bright spring day when he'd taken her for some of the famed ice cream on the little island in the middle of the Seine? She'd somehow managed to get ice cream on her cheek, and he had leant forward and swiped it off with his thumb. His eyes had linked to hers for one moment longer than she would have expected of a friend...

Maggie forced the thought away. This wasn't about her. Nor was the blame for that car accident something Raphael should shoulder. She could see where he was coming from. The number of times she'd asked herself whether or not her mother might have had just a few more months if she'd been the one at home caring for her...

She pressed her thumbs to her eyes and did her

best to squish the thoughts away. She watched Raphael tease at the aluminum wrapper holding his sandwich hostage. He looked about as interested in having lunch as she was. *Not very.*

She ducked her head and tried to catch his eye. "You know, people organize going out for supper all the time. That hardly makes you culpable. Road traffic accidents are just that. Accidents."

Raphael continued as if he hadn't heard her.

"Jean-Luc's wife and Amalie had been out of the city for the day and, as they were running late, had decided to drive in. Normally they would've taken the Métro." His voice grew hollow. "And then the accident happened."

"How did you find out?"

He looked her square in the eye. "The casualties were brought to our hospital. When Jean-Luc arrived I said he must stay with his wife in the recovery ward while they waited on news of Amalie. He was so frightened. I've never seen a man more terrified in my—" His voice caught in his throat.

Maggie dug her fingernails into her palms, forcing herself not to reach out for him. Every pore in her body ached to console him. To tell him it would be all right. But he didn't want comfort. She would have had to be blind not to see the torture that had become all but ingrained in his cell structure.

"He knew the protocol. He knew I was too close to Amalie to be her doctor. But he begged me to look after his little girl. To do everything I could. There were only junior surgeons available, and she had suffered severe internal trauma as well as massive blood loss by the time she reached the hospital."

"So…you were following his wishes." Maggie gave a little shake of the head. "I don't understand why you're torturing yourself."

He widened his eyes in disbelief, opened his palms wide and slammed them down on the table, sending shudders through their untouched meals. "I should have said no. I was too close."

"So why didn't you?"

The look he shot her told her he had asked himself the same thing again and again.

"We were short-staffed. Most of the other doctors on duty that day were less experienced— fresh out of medical school—and casualties from the accident were flooding in, one after the other. The senior surgeon on staff told me to find someone else, if I could, but there was no one I trusted with that precious life. My best friend's child."

The anguish in his voice was palpable, and despite the heat of the day Maggie wrapped her arms around herself to fend off the wave of shivers trickling down her spine.

"Had you been specifically told not to operate on her? Before you took Amalie into surgery, I mean?" Maggie wasn't sure why she'd asked the question, but getting everything in order seemed essential if she was to understand why Raphael was blaming himself for something that had patently been an awful accident.

He shook his head. No. He hadn't.

"I was a surgeon. A good one, I thought. I had vowed to do my very best—promised my dearest friend I would save his child—and when it came down to it I failed. I failed as a friend. I failed as a doctor. I failed a child. It is *my* fault his little girl died and I will carry the weight of that burden until the end of my days."

"And that's why you came here?"

He shook his head, not entirely understanding.

"To try and unload the burden…with distance?" she clarified.

He tipped his head back and forth.

"No. It's not so simple. I just—"

This was the moment he'd been over again and again. Doing the checklist. Ensuring he'd done everything he could to stabilize Amalie.

"My instinct was to stay, to see the surgery through right to the end, but there was another patient in the next room. They needed me to operate straight away. All that was left to do with Amalie was close up. An easy enough job for the junior surgeons."

"But...?"

"She went into cardiac arrest."

From the look on Maggie's face he knew he didn't need to spell out the lengths his team had gone to in their vain attempt to keep her alive.

"If I'd made the decision to stay in the room instead of rushing off to the next surgery she might have lived."

"*Might* have?"

"I'll never know."

He rattled through Amalie's injuries in detail. The surgical procedures he'd followed. The gut instinct that had told him to stay. The pragmatic override that had pulled him from the room.

"And the other patient? What happened with them?"

"They lived." He corrected himself. "*She*. She lived."

She'd even sent him flowers, with a note expressing her gratitude.

"So…" Maggie pressed her fingertips to her lips for a moment. "Africa? Vietnam? What was that for? Were you atoning, or something?"

Raphael considered Maggie for a moment before answering. He should tell her what Jean-Luc had said and the cutting effect his words had had.

All you do is take!

He'd felt… He'd actually felt *orphaned* after the Couttards had made it clear they weren't ready to see him and Jean-Luc had dismissed him with a flick of the hand. More so than when his actual parents had died. That was how precious his friendship had been. Jean-Luc and his parents had been his family.

"Go," Jean-Luc had said. "Go show what a big man you are somewhere else. You obviously know what is best. Who deserves your magic surgeon's hands. Your time. It must be so precious, your time. Please…" He'd stepped in close and said the last words so quietly Raphael had had to lean in to hear him. "Don't let me take one minute more of it."

And then he'd shut the door. Hadn't taken his calls. Raphael had no idea if he'd read the letters he'd written or torn them to shreds still in their envelopes.

"Things were difficult between me and Jean-Luc. His parents, too."

"What?" Maggie laughed. "They didn't banish you from France, did they?"

The black look that swept across his features suggested she wasn't far off the mark.

Raphael cleared his throat. "I needed to prove to myself I could still do it. Make a difference as a doctor."

"And did you?"

He shrugged. He'd been so emotionally absent he knew he hadn't made a difference on any sort of personal level, but as a doctor…yes. Yes, he had.

"So why are you here?"

He gave her his best Gallic shrug.

He wasn't ready to explain that it was Maggie he had sought. That she was the one person he believed would give him the most honest perspective on the type of man she thought he was. Mortal or monster.

He heard her muttering something under her breath.

"A quelque chose malheur est bon."

She remembered. It was a saying equivalent to *Every cloud has a silver lining.* Or, the more French interpretation, *Unhappiness is, at the very least, good for something.*

He'd used to say it when, inevitably, it had rained on one of their outings and they were forced to seek refuge under a small awning or in a tiny alcove. He'd always wondered if she'd ever cottoned on to the underlying meaning… Though it had rained, it had meant he could be closer to her.

"So." He clapped his hands together, the sound sharp against the white noise of the late-afternoon activity surrounding them. "I understand why you wouldn't want to work with me anymore. If you need to transfer me out, please… I completely understand."

"You have got to be absolutely joking me." Maggie shook her head back and forth.

This was a lot of information to take on board, but it certainly answered the bulk of her questions.

Raphael had been through the wringer. He'd

changed, all right. But he was truly trying to make himself a better man than he had been before this tragedy. He was living with an unanswerable question and it had obviously been hell.

Would the child have lived if he had made a different decision?

As little as she knew about surgery, she knew enough about the traumatic injuries Amalie had suffered to imagine the answer would be no. And he'd returned to medicine. That wasn't something a man who doubted his skills would do. There *had* to be something more. Something he hadn't yet come to terms with.

"It's okay." Raphael's accent thickened. "I wouldn't want to work with me either, after knowing the truth. I am sorry I wasn't more honest before I came—"

"No." Maggie stopped him with a hand gesture. "Are you *mad*? Now that I know what you've been through there isn't a chance in the universe I'd let you work with someone else."

He bridled and it pleased her to see there was still fire in his spirit. He wasn't beaten. Just lost.

"Cool your jets." She took a deep breath and put her hands up so she could take a moment to put her thoughts in order. "I'm not keeping you pinned to my side because I think you're a bad doctor. Or a liar. Or a disappointment. Or whatever other words you attack yourself with. I want to work with you because what you need more than anything after what you've been through is a friend."

A quizzical look passed across his features. "Why would you want to work with me after this? Trust me? You said at the beginning of this that people change. I am proof of this, Maggie. I have changed."

"Raphael Bouchon." She fixed him with a stern expression, hoping he was reading affection in her expression rather than someone passing judgment. "I know it's been a long time seen we've seen each other, but a man can't change *that* much. That young man I met in Paris was the most honest, honorable, kind person I had ever met. And, though an awful lot of water has passed under the bridge since then, I still believe that's true. You're still that young man. But with maybe just a bit more of a distinguished air."

She pointed to her temples trying to indicate that she liked the salt and pepper look working its way through his rich chestnut hair.

"No, Maggie. You are kind, but…" Raphael

opened his water bottle and took a long draught before continuing. "I thought when I saw you I would see the old me again. That I would find him somewhere buried in here." He made a fist and thumped it on his chest as he shook his head. "Now that I'm here, I see that you're just the same. But I don't think that seventeen-year-old Raphael you met all those years ago exists anymore. I'm not fun to be with. I can't see any point in looking forward to the future the way I once did. I don't even see the point of dreaming about the future. I failed my friend. I have the blood of a child on my hands. My best friend's child."

She shook her head—no, no, *no*—as a powerful rush of energy charged through her bloodstream.

If Raphael believed in their friendship enough to tell her about his darkest moments, she would show him just how strong her love for him was. Unrequited or otherwise.

If he needed a friend, he had one. If he needed a shoulder to cry on, she had two. If he wanted to believe in the possibility of love again…

She swallowed. That might be pushing things.

Baby steps.

She sucked in a deep breath of air and parted her lips. It was time to be as brave as Raphael.

"That's where you're wrong."

Wide blue eyes registered incredulity at her statement. "Maggie! I was *there*. I failed as a surgeon. I was the one who let Jean-Luc down. Let all the Couttards down."

"First things first."

She gave the picnic table a solid tap with her index finger, then wove her fingers together in front of her heart.

"I am very sorry for your loss. It must've been horrible for you. But you surely must see it was an impossible situation. And who's to say another surgeon might have made a different call? However cruel and personal it must feel, these things are random. It wasn't like you willed the fog to appear on that motorway or anything. And secondly—" she held up a hand so he would let her finish "—how exactly did you let Jean-Luc down? He asked you to do your best. To look after his little girl. I can't imagine you did anything other than try and save her."

Raphael looked at her, his features wreathed in disbelief. "Amalie *died*, Maggie."

She sat back and eyed him silently for a moment before taking another drink of her water.

Her heart ached for him. He was seeing the world through a distorted lens. One that showed him branded as a failure for not being omniscient. In that respect, yes, he *had* been too close to the patient. But in terms of deciding he didn't cut it as a surgeon...he'd just made it all up.

And then it hit her. All of the insecure dark thoughts she'd been having about Raphael not liking her, or thinking she was a loser, had also been a complete fiction. She'd seen what scared her most instead of stepping outside of herself and facing facts. It was something Raphael needed to do, too.

In that instant Maggie knew she would do everything in her power to help Raphael take off the blinkers that seemed unrelenting in their mission only to let him see the dark side.

The thought stopped her cold.

Had *she* worn the same blinkers with her father? Her brothers? Instead of being sexist, demanding, nineteen-fifties throwbacks, on a mission to keep her in a pinny, had they actually been as blindsided by her mum's death as she had?

They hadn't been in tears, or lost in faraway

thoughts or anything. It had seemed on the surface that everything was business as usual. But men were good at disguising things. Raphael being a perfect case in point.

But there was something else that was torturing him. Something beyond the failed surgery that he had yet to set right.

There were things *she* needed to set right as well.

When she'd come home to find her mother had been ill the entire time she'd been away, only to die while Maggie was flying home, Maggie's world had been turned upside down. At the time it had felt as though she'd been drowning in the past she had only just begun to escape. Blinded with grief and frustration, she'd blamed her brothers and her father for pushing her into the vacant role their mother had left behind. Carer. Cook. Cleaner. The very roles her mother had made her promise she would never take on.

But could it be that instead of being pushed she had willingly stepped into the spot her mother had once filled in their lives? That she had naturally found herself filling that void because she was the girl and that was what girls—*women*—did? Instead of it being a weak decision, perhaps she had been the only one strong enough to make sure their lives somehow returned to normal in the wake of their collective grief.

A strengthening weave of resolve unfurled within her. Raphael needed to believe he had been the only one strong enough to step into an impossible situation. If he could see that—know it in his heart—he would finally be able to forgive himself. He would finally be able to believe that, no matter who had operated on that poor little girl, her fate had already been decided when their car had been struck by another.

And if she wanted Raphael to believe that about himself she would have to take the same risk—and see her own life from another perspective.

"Maggie, please." Raphael raked his hands through his hair. "Put me out of my misery."

She looked at him as if seeing him for the first time. She'd been miles away. About a twelve-hour drive, in fact.

Maggie tipped her head to the side and wove her fingers together under her chin. "After this shift is over we've got four days off, right?"

He nodded.

"How would you feel about making it a bit longer?"

Maggie held her breath, waiting for his answer. Taking him home to meet her family was akin to unzipping her chest and handing him her heart. And then throwing some warts on top of the whole mess for good measure.

Raphael didn't look too pleased about the invitation.

"This isn't about you wanting me to be transferred to a different paramedic station, is it?"

"No! Crikey! No, not all."

"So we're good on that front?"

"Yeah! Of course. Now that I understand why you've been such a downer— I mean..."

To her relief, Raphael gave a self-deprecating laugh and held up his hands. "I *have* been a downer. But..." again that Gallic shrug "...now you know I have my reasons."

"I know. And it's a pretty big reason." She played with the edge of the aluminum wrapping on her sandwich and then, feeling a sudden hit of hunger, went ahead and unwrapped it. "Now that I know what's been going on in that head of yours..." she pointed her finger between the pair of them "...you and me? We're solid."

Maggie took an enormous bite of her sandwich and then grinned at him, a daub of sauce teasing at the crest of her upper lip before she swiped it away with her tongue.

He didn't deserve her. The open-hearted way in which Maggie had absorbed the worst thing he'd ever done in his life and simply...*accepted* it, forgiven him for the transgression and moved on.

It was humbling.

Maggie munched on a few crisps, then took a gulp of water. "So, back to me. Have you had your fill of being a tourist in Sydney?"

Raphael shrugged. The only reason he'd come to Australia was to see Maggie. So saying yes was an honest enough answer. And honesty was the only way forward. He saw that now.

"I think you and I need to go on a road trip. Get you out beyond the black stump."

Her tone was decisive. As if hearing his story had given her a new course of action. More to the point, her entire demeanor had changed...as if they were actually friends again.

"Black stump?"

"City limits," she explained, a soft flush coloring her cheeks. "If you say yes, there's a whole lot more Aussie slang waiting for you outside of Sydney. If you're feeling brave enough, that is."

Something in him softened. She was trying.

He'd been making this whole reunion thing tough. More than tough. And yet she was still trying.

"Are you sure this isn't some attempt to take me out to the desert with a flint and a bottle of water to see if I make it out alive? A survival of the Aussie-est?"

She shrugged and smiled. "We-e-ell..." She drew out the word. "Nah. Of course not. Look. I have to go out there. Family."

He lifted his eyebrows. She hadn't mentioned her family. Not once.

"A reunion?"

She shook her head. "No. But let's just say you're going to see a whole side of me you never knew existed if you say yes."

"Sounds intriguing." Was she trying to ease his guilt? Prove he wasn't alone?

Her features darkened.

"It's not a reunion, but... You've been incredibly honest with me and I appreciate it." She pressed her hands to the center of her chest. "From the very bottom of my heart. It proves to me our friendship meant as much to you as it did to me."

Raphael locked eyes with her. "It did. It still does."

He watched as she sucked in a tight breath, then made the decision to speak.

"I don't think you are responsible for Amalie's death."

He scrubbed his hands along his legs. "Maggie, you weren't there—"

"No. I know. But I know *you*. You made the best decision you could at the time. I've been watching you work and you have it. That ability to make a split-second decision about a patient that is going to be for their benefit. No matter what you think of yourself now, I know without a shadow of a doubt that you simply do not have it in you to let another human's life pass through your hands if it doesn't have to."

The words struck so deep Raphael knew they would be embossed on his heart forever. But Maggie didn't owe him this: an easy out. She didn't owe him anything.

"*Tu es trop gentile*, Maggie. I am so grateful to you for not...for not thinking the absolute worst of me."

"How could I?"

There were countless answers for that one. He

began totting them up before answering, then stopped himself. Holding back from Maggie had only meant making himself his own worst enemy. Could this be the first step in forgiving himself? Finding a way to claw himself out of the black hole he'd all but swan-dived in to?

He met her clear green eyes and saw nothing but compassion in them. Empathy. Her unfiltered gaze was the oasis of peace he'd been seeking all these months.

"I'm glad I came." He reached across and took her hand in his, stroking his thumb along the back of it.

"Me, too." She gave him a shy smile, thought for a minute, then winced. "But I do think…perhaps…you need to decide if your heart is really in the paramedic world."

"What?" He feigned affront. "You don't think I've been doing a good job?"

She gave a melodramatic sigh. For his benefit entirely.

"Quite the opposite. And you know that." She tugged her hand out of his and poked him in the arm. "But it's not where your *heart* is. A blind man could suss that one out. And although running around the world and showing off your medical prowess is an amazing thing to do, I don't think that's what you're doing. You're more... It's more like you're living life on the run. Waiting for that one medical save that will put you back to the place you were before that night. From where I'm sitting, what you're feeling is grief, not guilt. And you're not letting yourself be good old-fashioned sad. Maybe you should do that, instead of all this globetrotting."

She put on a dramatic television presenter's voice. "*'Dr. Raphael Bouchon has been spotted in yet another country. Paraguay this time. Or was it Brazil? Will he keep interested parties guessing as to his whereabouts for years to come? Or will he suck it up, go back to France, and have a weep and a talk with Jean-Luc? Will he finally make peace with his dearest friend?'* Apart from me, of course." She smirked.

Despite himself, he smiled.

"This isn't—" He stopped himself. It *was* running. All of it. He hadn't even fully unpacked his suitcase and he'd been in Australia over a month. Even "his" dog wasn't his. Just a stray he'd called Monster who helped him eat his leftovers.

He shrugged, accepting her comments as fair, and finally picked up his sandwich. "Are you saying you don't like the idea of me living as an outlaw in your fair city?"

She laughed and when their eyes met he knew she liked the idea of something, all right. But he was guessing it wasn't the outlaw thing.

A sting of regret that he hadn't kissed her all those years ago resurfaced.

An even bigger hit of remorse could so easily follow in its wake if he didn't get his act together and start to actively live his life. With purpose. With passion. With *love*.

Maggie put her sandwich down and took a sip of water.

"So, if you can scrape the bottom of your soul and put your darkest moments on display, why don't you take a break from beating yourself up about it and come out and see a bit of mine? The soul stuff I mean. The black parts."

"Just because I've done something awful it doesn't mean you—"

"Uh-uh!" She held up a hand. "I'm not done yet. I think this trip will be good for you. Maybe help you see life isn't always the way you think it is."

"You're talking in riddles."

"Yeah, well… I didn't exactly think I'd ever be telling you any of this."

"Any of what?"

She shook her head. "It's a show and tell sort of thing. You have to be there to understand."

Her eyes shifted up to the tree above them and glassed over. She shrugged her shoulder upward to swipe at the single tear snaking down her cheek and took another bite of sandwich. A poor disguise for an obvious rush of emotion.

When she'd finished chewing she swallowed, waved a hand as if erasing a whiteboard, and said, "Forget about all the 'feelings' stuff. It's a road trip—plain and simple. You are under no pressure to say yes. But at the very least, after we get past the Blue Mountains, you'll see first-hand that there is a whole lot of nothing in between the coasts of this fair isle. Besides, I need someone to keep me awake. It's a long drive."

There was something else. Something she wasn't saying. But he didn't press. He'd wanted a change and Maggie was delivering.

Maggie.

A life-affirming electrical current shot through him and the first undiluted desire simply to say yes to life took hold of his heart.

Maggie was the difference. He'd just told her about the worst moment in his life and already he felt…not lighter, exactly, but less alone. If Maggie could believe that one single shred of the man she'd met still existed…

"What?" Maggie's features scrunched up as she tried to interpret his expression. "You haven't gone soft on me, have you? Not up for a bit of rough and tumble out in the Woop Woop?"

"Quoi?"

"The Outback," she explained with a laugh. "The middle of nowhere."

He crossed his arms, narrowing his eyes in a dubious squint.

"Is this some sort of Australian ritual? Bringing a poor, defenseless Frenchman to the Outback to see if he can make his way back to civilization as a means of proving himself?"

"Something like that." The hint of a mysterious smile teased at the corner of her lips. "Or it could just be to prove you can survive a couple of days with my brothers. Believe me—if you can make it forty-eight hours straight with the Louis brothers, you can survive anything."

A warmth hit Raphael's heart, and with it came a sudden hunger. Nothing to do with being invited to meet the family of the girl he'd always wondered *What if?* about, he told himself drily.

He began unwrapping his sandwich, abruptly stopped and locked eyes with her.

"One question."

The change in his own voice surprised him. It reminded him of the man he'd used to be before the harshness of grief had turned him irritable. It was the voice of a man who *cared*.

"Can I bring my dog?"

Maggie's eyed widened and stayed wide as her radio crackled to life and a rapid-fire stream of instructions rattled through. "Code Twenty-one," she whispered, her green eyes locked on his as she continued listening.

Can I bring my dog?

What was *that* all about? It wasn't like Monster was actually *his*. Or that he needed a buffer between him and Maggie. She was…she was *Maggie*. The sunny-faced, flame-haired girl—

Who was pressing herself up and away from the picnic table, grabbing her half-eaten sandwich and making a "wheels up" spin with her finger as she continued to take down the details of their call-out.

It was at that moment that he truly saw her

for who she was. Maggie wasn't the lanky, shy, still-growing-into-her-skin teen he'd met thirteen years ago, who'd tied an invisible ribbon round his heart.

She was a woman.

And a beautiful one at that.

He'd been so preoccupied with shaking off the ghosts chasing him around the world that he hadn't stop to breathe her in. This past year he had felt as if he'd only just been holding on to the back of a runaway train, and now Maggie had leapt on and hit the brakes. Showed him there was more than one way to handle the grieving process he knew he had to go through.

"We've got a broken arm, a possible neck fracture, and a few more injuries."

"All for one patient?" He grabbed his own sandwich and drink, following her at a jog.

"No. Cheerleading pyramid gone wrong."

"Cheerleading?"

"Cheerleading. Or not, as the case may be," she added soberly, before jumping into the ambulance.

When they arrived at the high school they pulled into the car park at the same time as another am-

bulance. Maggie's mate Stevo and his new partner Casey. Raphael rolled down his window as a
man ran between the pair of vehicles, waving his
arms and identifying himself as the headmaster.

After a quick conference with the headmaster
they drove the ambulances round to the school's
large playing field to find a huge group of people
gathered in several circles.

"I'll grab the tib-fib compound," Stevo called,
heading for a group already opening up to let him
and his pale-faced junior through. Those injuries
had the potential to be pretty gory. Raphael felt
for Casey.

"She looks horrified, poor thing." Maggie made
a sympathetic noise, then grabbed a run bag and
a spine board. "Oh, well. There's only one way to
learn and that's by confronting the tough stuff.
Can you grab a couple of extra collars and a pile
of blankets? It looks like you and I are over here."

Maggie tipped her head at the pair of girls in
cheerleading outfits running toward them.

Confronting the tough stuff.

Precisely what *he* needed to do.

"Over here!" One of the cheerleaders arced her
arm and pointed toward a nearby group. "She
says she can't feel her legs!"

Raphael shouldered his run bag and set off in a jog alongside Maggie, hoping the situation wasn't as grim as it sounded. At the very least, the patient was alert. Speaking. From what he'd heard, cheerleading injuries could be catastrophic, with all the gymnastics involved.

Words whirled round him—"flyer", "base holders weren't there", "on her head"—as they approached the circle around a sixteen or seventeen-year-old girl. A hush fell upon the crowd.

"Hello, love." Maggie dropped down to her knees behind the girl and immediately stabilized her head by bracing her elbows on the ground and holding her temples steady. She shot Raphael a quick look, then shifted her gaze to the girl's legs. They were lying at peculiar angles and, whilst alert, the girl had an entirely mystified expression playing across her face.

"Looks like someone took cheerleading to some new heights—oops. No, no. Stay still, darlin'. We want to make sure we don't move anything we're not supposed to."

Maggie gave Raphael a nod and he ran a series of quick checks for additional injuries, keeping a sharp eye on the patient as he moved the teen's legs into place. No response.

"Have you seen anything your end? Spinal injuries? Brain?" He asked his questions in French, and a swift murmur of approbation followed from the teenagers behind him. If they knew he'd spoken in French to keep potentially bleak news from them, they wouldn't be saying such nice things.

Maggie shook her head. "Protocol says we should use the stiff neck braces for precautionary immobilization, but I think they're too much for her." Maggie held her hand alongside the girl's neck, as if measuring it.

"I think the vacuum mattress would be best. It will keep her entire body stabilized without any unnecessary jarring—particularly if she has a pelvic fracture."

Maggie's eyes flashed to his.

"We won't be able to see any internal bleeding, so the best we can do is stabilize her as much as possible."

Raphael's mind had ticked over to automatic pilot—which didn't second-guess his every decision. And it felt good. It felt like being a trauma doctor again.

Maggie tugged a couple of blankets off the pile Raphael had placed on the ground and started rolling them into boomerang shapes. "I'll use these to stabilize for now, while you do the rest of the checks."

After examining the girl for any immediate evidence of neck wounds or the potential for underlying hematomas, Raphael ran to get the mattress.

When he returned he saw Maggie checking the girl's vitals again. "Have you looked for signs of neurogenic shock?"

Maggie shook her head. "I've only just started. I've done a quick pulse check—doesn't seem too low. Or high, for that matter." She smiled down at her young charge. "All right, there, love? Seems as though your ticker's all right." Then, in a lower voice she continued. "Amazing...good. Not bradychardic in the slightest."

"What does that mean?" the girl asked.

"It means your body seems to be doing its best to help you recover." Maggie brushed her fingers along the girl's cheek, then rattled through a few stats with Raphael.

In between all the medical speak with Raphael, Maggie continued to keep up a steady flow of fact-gathering in the guise of casual chit-chat with their patient. This was her forte. He could see that now.

Being calm, warm and conversational kept the patient relaxed, the atmosphere less stressed, and significantly reduced the patient's potential for panic. His quest to be as exacting as he could had all but turned him into an automaton. A patient's worst nightmare.

He smiled as Maggie continued.

What was her name?

Jodi.

How long had she been a cheerleader?

Four years, and this was to have been her last as she was planning on becoming a veterinarian.

Any favorite animals?

Dogs. Definitely dogs.

Maggie shot him a quick look, so he threw in a comment about dogs being wonderful.

What pyramid routine had they been practicing?

The Eiffel Tower.

A pair of amused green eyes met his.

"Well, isn't that a coincidence?" Maggie put her hand directly above Jodi's eyeline. "Can you move your eyes toward the handsome chap over there on your left?" Maggie used her finger above the girl's face as a guideline.

Raphael smiled. That was a clever way to check her responses.

Wait a minute… *Handsome?*

"He's a genuine Frenchman, and—would you believe it?—the very same man who took me all bright-eyed and bushy-tailed around Paris. The first day we met he took me to see the Eiffel Tower."

Maggie's eyes flicked up to Raphael's and for a microscopic instant they caught and locked. Something in him flared hot and bright as he saw Maggie in full, glorious high-definition. The flame-colored hair. The beautiful green eyes. The milky white skin, flawless save a tiny scar at the corner of one of her eyes.

How had he not noticed that before? Had someone hurt her? Another swell of emotion built in him. A feeling of fierce protectiveness. If anyone had hurt Maggie he'd—

"Raphael?"

He cleared his throat and looked up at the sea of expectant faces. This was definitely *not* the time for flirting or thumping his chest like a he-man.

Had Maggie been flirting or just being nice?

"Um, Raph?" There were questions in Maggie's eyes, and not all of them were about work.

"*Alors*…shall we get Jodi onto the spine board?"

Raphael moved the board to Jodi's right, ensuring the vacuum mattress was in place, and on his count they rolled her onto the board and secured her with the series of straps attached to the mattress.

"How's your breathing, Jodi?" Raphael asked.

The teen stared at him, wide-eyed. "Say that again."

"How's your breathing?"

He shot an alarmed look in Maggie's direction. Breathing problems indicated much more serious injuries that might require intubation, the need for a positive-pressure bag-valve-mask device—though there were issues that went along with that as well. Distorting the airway could impair breathing, then circulation…

He was surprised to hear Maggie giggling.

"I think her breathing's just fine, Raphael. It's your accent. She likes it."

"And his name, too." Jodi's voice was positively dreamy and her expression fully doe-eyed.

"Oops! Easy, love—let's keep you looking straight up. Even if it's just *my* old mug you're looking at."

Maggie quickly pushed the blankets back into

place, realigning Jodi's head to a neutral anatomical position. She widened her middle and index fingers between the girl's chin and suprasternal notch to get a measurement.

"Maybe we'd better slip an extra-small soft collar on her for the journey. Especially…" Maggie dropped a teasing wink at Raphael "…as you're the one who's going to be sitting in the back of the ambulance with our girl, here."

Raphael laughed and together, with the quick efficiency that usually came from years of working together, they inflated the mattress, lifted Jodi onto the wheeled gurney and loaded her into the ambulance for their ride to the hospital.

A few hours and several patients later they were sitting in companionable silence at the front of the ambulance as they headed back to the station.

Raphael's thoughts returned to Maggie's invitation.

"Did you mean it?" His voice sounded more intense than he'd anticipated. Pulling back the emotion, he clarified, "About the road trip?"

Maggie threw him a quick look, the bulk of her attention on the rush hour traffic she was battling. "Yeah, I suppose…"

"That doesn't sound as if you've entirely made up your mind. If it was a charity invitation—"

"No, no." She batted a hand between them. "That wasn't it at all. It's just that it's a long way. *Aussie* long. I thought it might be part of your How-to-be-an-Australian training, but if you don't plan on sticking around it might be too much bother."

He dropped his head and looked at his hands.

Why was he here?

To see Maggie.

Why did he want to see Maggie?

To find out if a human heart still pounded in his chest.

What happened when he was with Maggie?

Blood charged through his veins.

"Sounds good. I'd like to do it."

She threw him a quick glance. "All right, then. Well, in that case, the invitation is still open— but it comes with a warning."

"Are there venomous snakes where we are going?"

She laughed. "Loads. But they're everywhere in Australia. The warning is much bigger. My brothers can't cook for toffee. Chances are you're going to have to eat whatever I manage to rustle up—and let's just say most of the takeaways near my flat would go out of business if I moved."

"Didn't your mother cook?"

His mother's cooking was one of his better memories of his home life, but from the chill that instantly descended between them, it was obviously not the right question to ask Maggie.

"She did." Maggie's voice sounded hollow. "Best cook in town."

"Did?"

"She passed a while back."

"I'm sorry to hear that."

She made a small noise, her gaze fastidiously trained on the cars in front of them, each battling for those few precious centimeters taking them that much closer to home.

Home.

Such a simple word, but one laden with the power of a nuclear bomb.

He didn't know where home *was* anymore. He'd rented expensive modern apartments in Paris. A total contrast to the cramped, low-rent housing he had grown up in with his parents. A tent in Africa. A tiny beach house here in Sydney.

Nothing seemed to fit.

The thought twisted and tightened in his gut.

Would anything? Anywhere? Would yet another trip finally give him some answers?

He looked out of the window as they crawled past one of Sydney's most famous beaches. It was mid-week but the shore was packed with families, couples, surfers, sun-worshippers. The sky was a beautiful, crisp blue. The air was tinged with a lightly salted tang. It was heaven on earth, and yet he still felt as though being a part of it all remained out of reach. Impossibly so.

He looked across to Maggie, startled to see her swipe at the film of tears blurring her clear green eyes. The moment was over so quickly he wondered if he'd imagined it. And in its place was her bright, ready smile as the radio crackled to life with a call-out to an asthma attack.

She flicked on the blue lights.

"Let's hit one more before we call it quits, shall we?"

CHAPTER SEVEN

Don't forget the socks, Dags.

MAGGIE GROWLED A response at the text message, half tempted to throw her phone out the car window. But she knew she'd go to the store. Buy the socks. Take the washing powder. Make the meat pies. Enough to put in the freezer for later.

She could already see herself rolling up her sleeves and cleaning up the three months' worth of detritus that had no doubt accrued in the Louis household.

It was what she did. It was what *they* did. Annoying as they were, at least she *had* a family. It was a lot more than Raphael had.

Losing the Couttards had genuinely seemed to set him adrift.

Not that she'd gone over the reasons he'd chosen to seek her out a thousand times, or anything, but…had he come to fill a void? One that Jean-

Luc and his parents had filled when they were teens?

Losing Jean-Luc as a friend must have been devastating for him.

When she'd lost her mother she had felt as if the world had disappeared from beneath her feet. But that was cancer. Just one of life's cruel turns.

Losing a friend…losing a child.

The thought gave her chills. Raphael's loss was a vivid reminder that, even if they *did* drive her bonkers, her father and brothers had been there for her all along. The proverbial wind beneath her wings.

She glared at her phone for a minute, then felt her features soften as she punched in a reply.

I've already put holes in the big toes. Just the way you like 'em. x PS Don't call me Dags. I'm bringing a friend. Who has manners.

Another message pinged straight back. Something about bringing extra "talent" into town for the brothers' pleasure which she chose to ignore. There was no chance she'd bring a *female* friend out to meet that lot of larrikins. Kelly had once begged her and she'd flat-out refused.

Besides, if she explained to her brothers that her "friend" was actually the man she was trying to convince herself she wasn't head over heels in love with, her phone might blow up with their responses.

And it wasn't as if it was reciprocated. If Raphael had actually come to Oz because he was in love with her it would've come out by now.

So it was Just Friends, then. And that was the way the biscuit was bashed.

The instant Maggie laid eyes on Raphael the next morning her tummy went all fluttery butterfly park, and she knew the talking-to she'd given herself about the whole Just Friends thing had been entirely unsuccessful.

He was already out on the street, lit by a single lamppost in the pre-dawn gloaming, his hair scruffy, blue eyes still a bit sleepy, his trousers hanging on his slim hips, a soft navy blue chambray shirt making the most of his shoulders and trim build—well, it *looked* soft. Not to mention the just-about-as-adorable-as-they-came dog by his side.

Raphael with a hang-dog pooch? That image

all but nailed Raphael's place in her affections for evermore.

If he hadn't spied her—unleashing one of those bright smiles of his that had the power to make the world a better place—she would've spent a few minutes banging her head against the steering wheel. Doomed! That was what she was. Doomed to be a spinster forever. Lost to an unrequited love that would never blossom in a million years.

What had she been thinking? A fourteen-hour road trip with the most gorgeous man in the universe and his dog? If she came out of this with one single shred of dignity left intact it would be an out-and-out miracle. Particularly once he met her family.

Oh, *cuh-rikey*. This was a Class A brain failure.

She dropped her head to her steering wheel anyway, little flashes of ominous foreboding appearing in her mind's eye. One of her brothers' huge workman's hands crushing Raphael's beautiful surgeon's hands in a friendly *How-ya-going? Don't-you-dare-mess-with-my-sister* handshake. Their unrelenting passion for burnt snags on a barbie. The coolbox filled with a fresh slab of tinnies "just in case" it was a scorcher. It was *always* a scorcher.

Raphael would catch the first flight out of Broken Hill. If there even was one that day.

Was it too late to talk him out of it?

"Salut, Maggie. Ça va?"

The man had a voice like melted chocolate. What was she meant to say?

Why, yes, Raphael. I would be perfectly well—if inviting the only man I've ever loved to my crazy Outback family home were not the type of thing to send a girl stark raving mad. Which it is.

"Maggie?"

"Oui, ça va."

Sigh. Swirl. Flip. Loop-the-loop. A pop song clicked on in her head... If she could turn back time, indeed.

Raphael walked round to her car door and handed her a coffee through the open window. *"Un café* for my chauffeur..."

Before she could thank him, he passed her a beautiful eggshell-blue box with a cream ribbon around it.

"And a little something special for you."

An image of opening it and finding a diamond

ring flicked into her head, instantly unleashing a ridiculously huge explosion of tingles. Maybe fairy tales *did* come true…

"You didn't have to do this—"

"Of course I did." He waved away her protest. "I couldn't have you driving all the way across the state without some of Sydney's finest croissants."

His lips twisted into the inevitable Gallic *they're-not-French-but-they'll-do* twist, then melted into a smile.

"Yeah!" She rubbed her tummy in a show of gratitude, her heart sinking straight through to the foot well of the car.

Idiot.

Diamond ring.

Croissants. Of *course* the box had croissants in it.

Ah, well. Being a well-fed spinster was better than being one with a grumbling tummy.

She popped the box and the coffee into the central console between their seats and climbed out of the car.

"So this is Monster?" Maggie nodded down to the scruff-muffin who hadn't left Raphael's side.

The dog looked up at the pair of them, as if he knew he was the topic under discussion.

"Oui." Raphael hooked his fingers onto his hips and looked down at him with a warm smile. "He seems to have adopted me."

"Smart dog," Maggie said before she could think better of it.

Nice one, Mags. Why not just out-and-out tell the man you're completely in love with him?

Oh, mercy.

Was she?

Was the Pope Catholic? The sky blue? The earth beneath her as red as the blood pumping through her heart?

Yes. *Yes.* Near enough.

She hid her grimace of embarrassment as best she could as Raphael turned to her, his expression suddenly shadowed with sadness.

"Perhaps he is a little foolish. Pinning his hopes on a man who doesn't know if he is coming or going is never a wise investment."

Thunk. There went her heart. Plummeting straight down to the very center of the earth.

Her eyes lit on the harness in his hand. "Looks like you've made a bit of an investment in him."

"This?" Raphael held up the safety restraint

and smiled at it. "Yes. Perhaps it is me being hopeful."

"Hopeful is good." *Hopeful means you might stay.*

"Oui."

Raphael nodded, and their eyes connected so completely that Maggie was sure he could read her thoughts.

"Hopeful is good."

"Guess we'd better hit the road, then." Her voice came out more as a croak then a chirp. "You'll want to make the most of the time you two have together."

She scurried to the rear passenger door and opened it up so Raphael could secure Monster to the buckles and harness, all the while thinking, *Nice cover.* Way to show the man it would be a dream come true if he stuck around. Stayed a while.

And by "a while" she meant forever…

Raphael was marveling at how different the landscape was already. Fewer than a handful of hours outside of Sydney, they were working their way through the Blue Mountains. The vistas were utterly breathtaking. Unlike anything he'd seen before. And the atmosphere in the car was nice. A bit of chat. A bit of silence. Repeat.

"Maggie, this may seem like a silly question, but with a trip this long…in France we would fly or take a train. Why do you drive?"

"What?" Maggie shrugged away his question. "You never drove anywhere in France?"

"Of course—but not almost twelve hundred kilometers for a short visit."

Maggie tipped her head to the side and considered her response.

He smiled. She'd done that as a teen as well. Usually the questions had been about algebra or advanced chemistry. Those two thick fire-red plaits she'd always worn had shifted across her shoulders as she'd tipped her chin up to the left, her green eyes following suit until she gave her answer.

"I suppose… Oh, I don't know… It gives me a sense of being in control of my destiny."

"Driving for over a thousand kilometers?" He laughed. "So *that's* the answer to taking charge of your destiny. *Bof…*" He let out a low whistle. "If only I'd known."

If only it was that simple. He would've driven

ten…a hundred thousand kilometers if it would have changed things.

A thought struck him. He couldn't change the past. But he could change the future.

He reached his arm back between the seats and gave Monster a scratch behind the ears. The dog nestled into his hand. Trusting. Believing there was a future.

He looked across to Maggie, her eyes firmly on the road. He had a dog and a friend. A dear friend who…who maybe held the promise of something more?

"Holding the steering wheel of destiny is a personal thing." Maggie tip-tapped her fingers along the steering wheel, as if divining good advice. "Everybody's got their own thing, right? The thing that lets them soar. Perhaps you just haven't found yours yet. Besides…" she laughed "…it's not as if driving from Sydney to Broken Hill a dozen times has landed me a gold-plated mansion by the sea and the love of my life or anything!" She gave another horsey laugh, then quickly swallowed it.

"Is that what the goal is? A gold-plated mansion?"

She huffed out another laugh and gave him a

look as if he'd just turned into a stranger. "Yeah. That'd be about right. You read me like a book."

Raphael turned in his seat and looked at her. She was obviously being sarcastic. Of course she had zero designs on a gold-plated mansion, but...the love of her life? Something told him she meant *that* part. She was ready for love.

He was tempted to say something—crack a feeble joke and tell her that if a slightly the worse for wear heart was what she was after, his was all hers—when Maggie picked up the conversation again.

"Buses, trains, airplanes...they're just...you can't *do* anything if they're running late, you know? If you're driving then you get to be in charge. Pick your speed. Choose the route. Stop. Start. Do what you like, when you like, so you can get where you need to go exactly when you want to."

"Is that why you like driving the ambulance?"

"A little bit." She tipped her head back and forth, letting the idea settle, then smiled broadly. "A lot, actually. Even more so than my 'civilian' car, because I've got the lights, the siren. If they invented one that would let me drive above the traffic I'd be the happiest girl in Sydney."

She looked just like a little girl as she imagined the scenario. Which made him wonder if the answer wasn't, in fact, a simple one. "Does your desire to be mistress of your own time spring from always being late for things as a child?"

"No." She shook her head emphatically. "But I was late for something once…"

Maggie's sentence trailed off into nothing and the vibe coming from her distinctly said, *Time to back off,* mon ami.

He understood that feeling well enough, so he settled back into his seat and scanned the views spreading out beyond them—a rich palate of rusty cliff-sides, greens and blues still alight with the golden glow of the morning sun.

"If the rest of the journey is anything like this, I completely understand you wanting to be the master of your own destiny."

"It's pretty beautiful, isn't it?" Maggie said proudly.

"I didn't realize there were so many wineries near to the city."

Maggie nodded, much more relaxed now they'd shifted conversation topic. Playing tour guide suited her, and it was enjoyable to see her visible pride about all that her nation had to offer.

"We could've gone through the Hunter Valley, but that would've added a couple hundred kilometers to the trip. Really we could travel for weeks—months, even—and not get across to Perth. Australia's awash with wineries. Maybe not as many as France, but Aussies definitely like their wine." She laughed at a sudden memory. "Do you remember when you took me to that one cafe?"

They'd been to a lot of cafés and bistros, but a picture sprang to mind of a little corner café they had visited early on in her trip. It had been the French cliché. Cast-iron tables—a bit wobbly, with green tops. Rattan-framed bistro chairs with a blue and cream weave. A sun-bleached red awning beneath which the ubiquitous rude waiting staff jostled between the tightly packed tables. He'd been showing off. Acting the sophisticate for his New World charge.

Falling in love.

"Do you mean the café where we were served wine by that waiter who thought he was a model?"

"Exactly." Maggie laughed again, her green eyes sparking at the memory. "I was too embarrassed to tell you, but I'd never had wine before. Only stolen a few sips of my brothers' beer. I loved those little glasses so much…you know, the bistro glasses…but I didn't have a clue if I was doing anything right. I was amazed it was even legal!"

She sighed, and from the expression on her face he imagined even more memories were flooding in.

"Want to hear a confession?"

"Definitely. Yes." She shot him one of those bright smiles of hers that always seemed to land in the center of his heart.

"It was my first time, too."

She turned to him, features wide with astonishment. "*No.* I don't believe that for a second. Compared to me, you were so suave and sophisticated."

"Were?" he teased. He'd never felt suave or sophisticated for a single day of his life.

"Are," she parried solidly. "Believe me, when you see where I've come from you will see for a fact that you are, hands down, the most sophisticated person I know."

"Maggie Louis," he reprimanded her playfully. "You are being ridiculous. I am just a kid who was lucky enough to be born in a beautiful city. I wanted to show it off to you."

"You did that all right…" Her voice drifted off. "But I don't agree with you about the 'lucky kid' thing. You knew everything about Paris. I never felt for a single moment that I wasn't with the perfect person."

Her eyes flicked across to him and then quickly returned to the road, her upper teeth taking purchase on her lower lip as if she'd admitted more than she'd wanted to.

"I had a wonderful time showing you Paris."

He meant it to his very marrow. Going home to two parents more interested in the next bottle of spirits or who would win the inevitable fight over who'd spent the last of the welfare check had been a lot less fun than seeing Maggie's eyes light up when he showed her the nooks and crannies of Paris he'd discovered on the endless walks he'd taken to avoid going home.

"The truth is…" Maggie began slowly, then continued in a rush as if she'd dared herself to finish. "I think I was always a bit in love with you."

The instant she'd said it a thousand memories fell into place. The gentle looks. The soft smiles. Those moments when their hands or fingers had brushed and it had felt as though time itself had decided to stand still.

It was blatantly obvious that Maggie couldn't take it back fast enough. Words began tumbling out to erase what she'd said.

Of course only in a schoolgirl kind of way…a teenage crush…ridiculous…nothing to worry about. He mustn't think he was trapped in the car with her…she wasn't a stalker or anything."

"Maggie! *Arrêts.* It's okay. We were kids. Besides, even if I'd wanted to I couldn't have done anything about it."

Her lids lowered to half-mast and she shot him a look.

"Jean-Luc," he said as a means of explanation. *Tell her! Tell her you felt the same way!*

She lifted a finger and rolled it round. *Keep on talking,* it said. Clearly just saying Jean-Luc's name wasn't enough.

He sucked in a deep breath. Talking about Jean-Luc in any capacity was tough. Going back to the "good old days" was the hardest. Because they seemed the furthest out of reach.

"He told me he'd give me a black eye if I even so much as *thought* of kissing you."

"He did?"

Raphael nodded. "He did."

"And you listened to him?" Maggie gave him a quick glance.

"Let's just say Jean-Luc was acting at his mother's behest."

"Um…" Maggie's voice sounded dubious. "Since when do teenage boys listen to their mother? I grew up with three brothers, remember?"

"If one of your brothers had threatened someone who had designs on you with a black eye, would the boy have listened?"

Maggie obviously didn't need long to work that one out.

"Most likely—but that's small town stuff. Jean-Luc was your best friend. And he already *had* a girlfriend. Surely he would've just ignored his mother and told you to go for it?"

"Is that what you would have liked?"

"Raphael." Maggie threw him a stern look. "This is already immensely embarrassing. I'm not going to beg you to explain to me why you never kissed me."

There were a thousand reasons why. How did he explain to her that the Couttards had been his second family? That they had provided the structure and the balance—and sometimes the square meals—he had needed throughout his teens.

It had been out of loyalty. Maggie would understand that. And yet every part of him wished he had taken the risk.

"I know it sounds a bit pathetic, but think about it. Would *you* have disobeyed Madame Couttard?"

Maggie's features stayed static as she considered the question. "No. Definitely not. She was lovely, but she was a stern woman. I remember every time I asked why they ate so late she would fix me with an astonished expression, pop her hands on her hips and say. *'Je n'aime pas manger avec les poules, Margaret!'*"

"Exactly." Raphael tapped the dashboard soundly. "She saw being your host mother as akin to being your *own* mother. Looking out for you. Caring for you. Making sure errant teenage French boys didn't get any wayward ideas. The only change she wanted in you when she returned you to your own mother was speaking better French."

Maggie nodded and made an undefinable noise. "Yeah, well…my French certainly improved, all right."

She pushed a button on the display panel and turned on the radio.

Topic. Closed.

A brick wall to bang his head on would be useful about now.

Ça me soûle!

He scrubbed a hand through his hair and looked out of the window. Well, that had been about the quickest way to go from awkward to awful. The perfect tone to set for a road trip lasting over a thousand kilometers. *Très bien.*

Just say something to make her feel better about you not kissing her when you should have.

"It was a long time ago."

Nice. Exactly what she wanted to hear. That her feelings were silly and adolescent.

"Yeah. It *was* a long time ago." She nodded, cheeks flaming with embarrassment. "Would you—? Would you just…just forget I said anything? All right?"

She was gripping the steering wheel so hard her hands were trembling. Her eyes were glued to the curve of the mountainous roads ahead of them as if her life depended on it.

With every pore of his body Raphael ached for things to be different.

And that was precisely the moment when Raphael knew why he'd come to Australia.

Not to find himself. Not to make peace with his past. It was to find Maggie. To see if he could put a name to that elusive *something* that floated around in his heart whenever he thought of her.

She'd named it first. It was love.

Maggie held up her ice cream cone and tipped it towards Raphael's wattleseed flavored scoop for a "cheers" bump.

"So this is the world's best ice cream?"

"Don't look so dubious. This town may not look like much, but when you're about five hundred kilometers from civilization it's the height of sophistication."

Maggie took a satisfyingly cold lick of her salt-bush and caramel cone. Ice cream fixed everything. Even incredibly awkward atmospheres in a car after you'd confessed to the man of your dreams that you've loved him since you were a teen and he's told you that someone's mom told him not to kiss you.

What she *should* be taking away from the whole mortifying scenario was the fact that Raphael had, for at least a nanosecond on the universe's timeline, *wanted* to kiss her. Not be sulking about having great French and no mother to show it off to. It wasn't as if she could change anything now.

Besides, if the *chaussure* had been on the other foot and *her* mother had laid down a similar order…

No pashing on the French exchange student, love. We've got to return that boy to his mother the way we found him.

Pffft.

She would have obeyed, too. Small town kids knew that parents talked. Nothing was a secret.

Except that her mother had already been dying of cancer the day Maggie had boarded a plane for Europe.

Raphael "clinked" her ice cream cone again. "You're right. This is excellent. I have to confess, finding a gelateria in a petrol station is not something I thought would happen today."

He was handing her an olive branch. Trying to get rid of the weirdness as well. So it looked as if they'd be friends forever.

If it was good enough for Ingrid Bergman and Humphrey Bogart…

Maggie gave him a *Strange things happen in Oz* shrug and a grin. "There are loads of Italians who settled in Australia, so the country definitely does good ice cream—wherever you are."

"As good as France?" Raphael arched a prideful brow.

Ruddy French. Not *everything* was better over there!

"I would bet you any amount of money in the universe they don't have wattleseed ice cream in Paris."

Raphael laughed. "You are probably right about that." He took a lick and made *mmm* noises as he swirled the entire tip of the cone between his parted lips.

Maggie tried not to stare. *Too much.*

"It's good. Tastes a bit like coffee. Would you like to try?"

"Yes, please." She leaned forward and took a lick, vividly aware of Raphael's eyes upon her. Was there something…*different* about the way he was watching her? Something softer?

The man was now aware that she'd been in love with him forever and a day…

Or maybe she had dirt on her face.

Whatever it was, his gaze was making her flush.

"Mmm. That's good. Want to try mine?"

Maggie held up her cone, felt her eyes going into some sort of crazy blinking fit as once again—almost in slow motion—his lips parted before surrounding the top of her cone and taking a small taste.

Her breath caught in her throat as she imagined the cold ice cream hitting his warm tongue, melting and swirling in his mouth. Hot darts of desire shot across her more intimate regions as he made that delicious noise again. He looked up at her through dark lashes with those beautiful blue eyes of his, and in that instant she felt as though her skin was on fire.

He wasn't even *touching* her and she was on fire.

Gulp.

She still loved him.

No, she didn't.

She *lusted* after him.

Loving someone meant knowing them, and she was about as far from knowing what made Raphael tick these days as she was from knowing how to fly a jumbo jet.

Road trips were fun only if you weren't dying of humiliation at the same time. This was obviously a mistake.

Even if Raphael *was* still gazing at her with that beautiful soft smile on his lips.

She started when he reached forward and tucked a wayward strand of hair behind her ear, his fingers softly grazing the side of her neck as they passed. It was all she could do not to groan with pleasure.

What would she do when they finally kissed?

You're not going to kiss!

Madame Couttard had made sure of that.

Pah!

If they kissed then she'd be completely in love with him—which was stupid because they were heading for Broken Hill and her mad-as-a-sack-of-frogs family.

When they arrived Raphael would find out who she was and what sort of place she came from. A universe away from his own background. The whole charade of being someone she wasn't would come to an abrupt end, her heart would break into a million tiny pieces and then they could all get on with their lives. Which would be a good thing.

Except right here, right now, Raphael was licking a little bit of wattleseed off of his lip and was inches away. If she moved her ice cream cone a tiny bit to the right and went up on tiptoe…

"Maggie? Is that your phone ringing?"

The hum and rush of desire dropped from Maggie's internal soundtrack and was replaced by the very clear chirruping of her ringtone.

Mortified that she'd been staring at Raphael all goofy-eyed and lovestruck, she turned away and pulled her phone from her small bag. It was Cyclops.

"What's up, mate? I'm out in the Woop Woop."

"Yeah, I know."

Cyclops' voice was in full business mode. *Uh-oh.*

"There's been a car crash reported between Cobar and Wilcannia. Coupla lorries and some secondary vehicles. Quite a few, from the sounds of it."

She listened intently as he detailed the location.

"You anywhere near there?"

Maggie closed her eyes and pictured the road. "We're about ten kilometers east, give or take. Is anyone else on the way?"

"Yeah. They're sending a chopper out from the Blues, but it'll take at least an hour to get it crewed up and in the air. The fire crews in Cobar are all out on other jobs, but I'm coming in a chaser air ambulance. Probably two hours out. The coppers are on their way. I think they're trying to send a fire crew in with some Jaws of Life, but they'll all be volunteers. Not sure how up on first aid they'll be. It sounds serious. Any chance you can get to them and help until we arrive? Got any gear on you? Is Frenchie with you?"

"Yes, yes and yes." She looked at Raphael and gave him a tight nod. "I've got a small run bag in the boot, but not much else. Hang on a second, Cyclops."

She took the phone away from her ear, tugged a couple of notes out of her pocket and handed them to Raphael.

"Do you mind grabbing a few extra bottles of water from the guys in the shop? Loads, in fact. And as much paper toweling as you can get. Tell them it's for a medical emergency. Car crash up the road."

Raphael's features tightened instantly, and the all too familiar clouding of the bright blue in his eyes shifted into place.

This was difficult terrain for him, given his recent history, but it was an emergency. And it was what Australian paramedics did. They mucked in when there was no one else.

He was gone before she had a chance to ask if he was up to it.

Good.

Maybe working on the ambos was helping take the edge off the guilt he felt.

You couldn't save everyone, she thought as she signed off with Cyclops, grabbed her medical kit from the boot and threw it in the back alongside a perplexed-looking Monster.

But you sure could try.

CHAPTER EIGHT

RAPHAEL SAW THE smoke before the vehicles came into view. These weren't his first crash victims since he'd left Paris, but it was the first time he'd been on-site at a multi-vehicle accident. Adding scent and sound to a scene he'd imagined again and again might be torture. Or it might be the first step in putting the past right.

A couple of kilometers down the road cars were already starting to tail back on the wide highway.

"I don't suppose you have a spare set of blue lights in your car?" Raphael asked rhetorically.

Maggie shook her head. "No. But I do have a red and blue top in my bag on the back seat, if Monster hasn't turned it into a bed. Do you mind digging through my things to find it? Hopefully it's not too near my undies." She shot him an apologetic smile.

He shook his head and smiled. Trust Maggie to problem-solve her way out of a situation other people would duck out of at the first hurdle.

"Here it is." He held out a red shirt with blue polka dots.

"Right. Your job is to hold that thing out of the window."

"What for?"

She yanked the car brusquely out of the slowing traffic and onto the hard shoulder. "Tell Monster to cover his ears. You're the lights. I'm the siren."

Clamping her lips together with a determined expression, Maggie pressed on the horn of her car with one hand and gunned the car down the hard shoulder with the other.

It was impossible not to be impressed.

He ventured a guess. "Older brothers?"

"Got it in one." She flashed him a smile. "As I said, there wasn't much to do in Broken Hill as a girl."

When they were close enough to start picking out details, Raphael's gut told him the next few hours were going to be grim.

"You ready for this?" Maggie's tone suggested she didn't really care if he was or he wasn't. Either way, he'd be rolling up his sleeves and getting to work.

"Of course. You can count on me."

He meant it, too. Medically, of course. But also

to support Maggie. The last thing he wanted was for her to have to worry about if he'd be all right on the accident scene.

"Why don't you have a dig around the medical kit and familiarize yourself with what we have? From the sound of things, we'll have to make it last for about an hour. Criticals first." She gave him an apologetic smile. "Sorry. I forget you're hardly a stranger to trauma. Talking it through before I arrive always helps me calm down."

"*Bien.* Talk away."

He secured the blue and red top between the window and the window frame, keeping half an ear on Maggie's ideas for the best tactical approach as he pulled her medical kit onto his lap and had a quick run through it. Rather than the handful of plasters and couple of bandages he had been expecting, it was a proper first responder bag, full of wound dressings, burn gels, eye gels, thermal blankets, Epi-pens—the lot.

"I like your version of a 'small' kit."

"Things happen out in the Woop Woop." Her eyes remained glued to the road. "There's also a couple of picnic rugs in the back. No doubt some of the other drivers will have them as well. Blankets are going to be our stretchers, our braces… just about everything until the choppers arrive."

Raphael nodded. Though it wasn't as good as having an ambulance's worth of gear, for some of these people the difference between no equipment and this soft bag could be critical.

Maggie slowed as they approached the jack-knifed road train. Its accordioned cab was enough to produce shivers. The trailers lay sprawled across the highway amidst a tangle of combis, caravans and utility vehicles—or utes, as the Australians called them.

When they pulled up at the apex of the crash Maggie was pure business.

A police car was already on the scene and she quickly identified herself and Raphael, offering to start setting up a triage area on the side of the road farthest away from the smoking vehicles.

"That'd be great." The officer introduced her to a nearby female in uniform and pointed them toward a spot they'd already pre-identified as being appropriate for triage. He lifted his chin towards Raphael. "You're a doctor?"

He nodded.

"Good. Come with me."

After rolling down the windows of the car and

pouring Monster a bowl of water, he shouldered the medical bag and jogged along after the policeman to the other side of the road train.

"We need as many people as possible. There's a motorcyclist who landed under a ute when he was skidding to a halt. Bloody miracle he's still alive. Don't think he's conscious, though. Hasn't said a word."

They rounded the corner. About ten people in crouching positions surrounded a mid-sized car still smoking from a recently doused engine fire.

"Quel desastre!"

The officer shot him a sideways glance. "You're not from around here, are ya?"

"France."

He let out a low whistle. "Well, this is a far cry from France, mate. Prepare to get sweaty. If we lift this ute on a three count are you good to pull him out?"

The officer had a couple of people shifting the vehicle, including the ashen-faced male driver who looked close to fainting. Raphael made a quick mental note to find him later and check for symptoms of shock or whiplash, then knelt down to see where the motorcyclist was. His lips thinned when he saw just how much of the vehicle's undercarriage was resting on his chest. He slipped two fingers beneath the man's helmet to check for a pulse. Thready. But it was there.

"Okay." He looked up at the officer, feeling his adrenaline kick in. "Whenever you are ready."

The three count came fast.

"Now—*lift*!"

Amidst the groans and grunts of exertion Raphael channeled his strength into a swift and fluid move, pulling the motorcyclist out and away from the undercarriage of the ute.

Leaving the biker's helmet on, he flicked the visor up, unsurprised to see the man was unconscious, a blue tinge appearing on his lips. Raphael dropped his gaze to his chest, taking in the depth, rate and symmetry of his chest as he struggled to breathe. The shallow, jagged breaths suggested a pneumothorax or flail chest.

It was difficult to tell what had happened without taking off his leathers. But taking off the leathers would come with its own set of complications. In a worst-case scenario the motorcycle gear might be the only thing holding together compound fractures and preventing massive blood loss. But palpating the man's chest with them on was pointless.

His brain kicked up to high gear.

"Can I get a couple extra pairs of hands, please?"

Protocol in France dictated leaving the helmet on, so he did. On his instructions, a pair of bystanders rolled the man onto a thermal blanket from Maggie's medical kit and, with their help, he carried him away from the site to the triage area Maggie had magicked out of nothing.

Most of the color coding seemed to come in the form of pieces of colorful fabrics secured to the white road reflectors on the edge of the hard shoulder.

Maggie appeared by his side. "What've you got?"

"Possible pneumothorax. Do you have any fourteen-gauge needles in there?" He nodded to the run bag. "His lung will need decompressing. It'll keep him stable—"

"For up to four hours," Maggie finished for him. "When you've done that are you happy to attend the patients still in their vehicles?"

Raphael nodded, taking a fraction of a second longer than he needed to search her eyes for any doubt in his ability. But, no. She was already pawing through the medical kit for the equipment he'd need for decompression.

Faith. Loyalty.

Two of Maggie's standout qualities. A shot of pride surged through him. Maggie believed in him. She trusted him in spite of everything she knew about him. It meant more to him than he'd expected. All he wanted to do now was make sure he kept it. Earned it. Sustained her belief in him as a doctor. As a man.

With the help of one of the women who'd carried the man over he quickly rolled thick supports to place on either side of the motorcyclist.

Once satisfied the patient was supported, he unzipped his leather jacket and inserted the fourteen-gauge needle, his head tipped to the man's lips as he waited for the return of steady breathing.

Beat. Beat. And breathing returned.

"Is he going to be all right?" The woman who had helped carry him over was still kneeling on the other side of the motorcyclist.

"He should be." Raphael did a quick scan of the man's abdominal area. No blood. No obvious sign of other injuries. A miracle, really.

"Will you be all right to watch him?"

The woman nodded, yes, still wide-eyed from seeing the quick-fix release of air from the man's chest cavity.

With a renewed sense of determination Raphael set out again with the police officer, who seemed to have a good handle on all the people involved in the accident.

The rest of the afternoon passed in a blur of serious traumatic injuries and quick fixes.

Supplies were severely limited, forcing him to come up with an innovative way of stabilizing one particularly bad compound fracture.

"Oooooh…*maaaaaaate*! That really, *really*—"

Raphael blanked out the stream of blue language coming out of the middle-aged man's mouth.

He was lucky to be alive. He was lucky the volunteer fire crew had been able to cut him out of his car.

Raphael's features tightened as he tried to stem the flow of blood with the pile of assorted clothing and towels other drivers had been bringing to him.

This man would be lucky to keep his leg. Keeping the area clean, blood loss to a minimum and the rest of his organs functioning properly was paramount.

"Incoming!"

Calls signaling the arrival of the first helicopter began to ring out. Raphael used himself as a cover for the man, steeling himself for the screams of pain he knew would follow as he continued to keep pressure on the open wound.

"What you got here, mate?"

A uniformed doctor appeared by his side, with another doctor running behind with a stretcher.

"Compound tib-fib. Possible comminute fracture—but that's just from what I can see."

"Right." The heli-medics gave him a short nod and turned their focus to the patient. "We're gonna get you into town, cobber…take a look at that leg. Hope you're all right with— Whoops! He's losing consciousness. Let's get him on the chopper. On three."

Raphael helped with the transfer and, satisfied the man was in good hands, felt clear to move onto the next patient.

Steadily, swiftly, he worked his way through each of the patients who were unable to leave their vehicles—or hadn't done so yet.

The generosity of spirit amongst the drivers who were uninjured amazed him. Each time he brought a new patient to the triage area there were more sets of helping hands.

"Easy. You don't want to put any weight on it

if you can help it." Raphael was helping a teen-aged boy hobble towards the lower-grade triage area in the hope of getting some ice.

"Do you think I crushed it? I've got a footie match tomorrow. Do you think I'll be able to play?"

Before Raphael could answer a couple of men ran and scooped the lad into an actual armchair.

"We gotcha, mate."

They caught the surprise in Raphael's gaze.

"We've got a lorry-load of furniture we were moving to a charity store. Figured it would come in handy for you lot."

"What else you got in there?" the teen asked. "Is there a couch or a bed? I'm going to need to elevate and ice this baby if I'm going to play to-morrow."

Raphael couldn't help but laugh. "I don't think you will be playing tomorrow. Even if you ice it."

He knelt on the ground and lifted the boy's ankle up onto his knee, noting as he did so the sharp wince the boy tried to hide.

A quick examination and Raphael was close to certain the lad had suffered a pilon fracture. It would compromise his footie career for a while—if not forever—but without an X-ray there was no point in diminishing the boy's clear fighting spirit.

He rose to his feet as the other "furniture man" appeared with a footstool.

"Here you are, mate. Best we can do. The sofas are going for the ladies."

Raphael jogged over to the edge of the triage area where people who had portable ice boxes—including several huge ones—had made ice, tea towels—whatever they had to hand—available.

He brought a tea towel full of ice over to the boy.

"Who have we got here?" Maggie appeared from behind the chair with a notebook and pen in her hands.

"Charlie Broughton."

Raphael grinned as he watched the boy turn into a young man before his eyes, ratcheting up his flirt factor. Gone were the winces and groans of pain, and in their place was a broad smile and an extended hand.

"And you are…?"

Maggie gave him a quick smirk. "The woman who's going to get you a lift into the city. What do we have here? Sprain?"

Raphael shook his head. "He will need X-rays, definitely, but his injury is not critical."

"What? *Mate*..." Charlie looked at him, aghast. "The footie team is going to be absolutely furious if I'm not on the field—"

"The footie team is going to have to learn to do without you for a match," Maggie cut in as she leaned over and took a peek beneath Charlie's icepack. "Even if it is a sprain, there's no chance you're playing tomorrow."

"Well..." Charlie managed to make the word sound flirtatious. "Yes, ma'am." He gave her a wink and another smile.

Maggie laughed good-naturedly and started taking his details.

Raphael took a moment to grab some water and take in the scene.

People were handing round water and food. Their own small but increasingly useful first aid kits. A young girl had even "adopted" Monster to make sure he didn't overheat in the vehicle.

With rapidly dwindling resources, Raphael was being forced to rely on the spirit that had compelled him to choose medicine in the first place. Compassion. Skill. Dedication to helping people through their most vulnerable moments.

He felt like a doctor again.

And there was one person he had to thank for that.

A freckle-faced, green-eyed, redhead whose attention was now solidly with the newly arrived air ambulance teams and helicopter crews from Sydney.

She was pointing out the triage areas, handing across her notes as well as giving verbal handovers for each and every patient and details of the medicine they'd been given. Florence Nightingale had nothing on his girl.

His girl?

Mid-flow, Maggie looked across the crowds of people gathered on the roadside, met his gaze solidly...and smiled.

"Here." Raphael held out a cold bottle of water to Maggie as they walked back to her car. "I hope you have been taking your own words of wisdom to heart and staying hydrated."

"Oh, brilliant. And *cold*!" She pressed the bottle to her throat and gave a sigh of relief. "I always forget how much hotter it is out past the Blues."

She shifted the bottle to one sunburnt cheek

and then the other, only to realize Raphael had been watching her the entire time. She swigged down a few grateful gulps. When she lowered the bottle from her lips there was something in his gaze she hadn't seen before.

Curiosity.

And not a brother-sister, friend-friend curiosity either.

A rush of goose pimples rippled across her entire body.

"That was pretty intense. Are you all right after all that?" Though it was a dodge away from what she was really thinking, the question had been playing in the back of her mind all day. She might as well use it as a cover for the fact that all she wanted to do was jump the man and snog him senseless.

He nodded with an assurance that put her at ease. She'd seen a change in him today. Glimpses of the "old" Raphael. Assured, confident. And more than that. There had been genuine compassion in the care he'd provided for those people today. Not that frightening hollow look in his eyes.

Today he had been *present*. Today he had been the man she'd always imagined he would become.

She balanced the water bottle on the car bonnet and rubbed her hands along her arms. "Whoo! You'd think I had a bit of heatstroke from my body's reaction to that water."

She tried to laugh, but when her eyes caught with Raphael's again it died in her throat.

"Do you think you might? You were pushing it today."

Raphael took a step towards her that caught her by surprise. So much so that she stumble-stepped backwards, only to bump into the car.

"Do you feel dizzy?"

Again, Raphael closed the distance between them, his eyes searching hers for answers. Or for dilated pupils. Which he would definitely see. And that wasn't just because the sun was beginning to set behind him.

"Maggie," he persisted, "are you feeling unwell?"

Dizzy. Weak-kneed. And a bit dreamy-eyed.

"No." She tried to shake her head, but couldn't.

Raphael reached up and cupped her face between his hands, searching her features for symptoms. She knew he'd feel heat in her cheeks. An acceleration in her heart-rate. Her breath had become shallow, her lungs impossible to fill, because everything in that instant was... *Raphael*.

And then he was kissing her. Softly at first. Tentatively. As if asking for permission to continue.

He didn't need to ask twice.

Her lips parted as his kisses gained confidence. And when she felt the initial sweep of his tongue along her lower lip a soft whimper of pure longing hummed from her chest. As the kisses deepened their breath intermingled to exhilarating effect, as if they were at long last joined as one.

One of Raphael's hands dropped to Maggie's waist, firmly tugging her closer to him as he wove the fingers of his other hand into the thick fistful of hair at the base of her neck.

For thirteen years she'd wondered what it would be like to kiss him... It was even better than she could ever have imagined.

The kisses...his touch. Everything about him was sensual. Erotic in its simplicity of purpose. The culmination of a day's intense work was pared down to these perfectly intoxicating expressions of desire and pent-up longing.

At last she knew in her heart that he felt it too.

The kisses came in so many variations it was

impossible to keep track. Some were so passionate she thought her heart wouldn't be able to keep up and others were so exquisitely tender she could hardly breathe.

The world had long since blurred around them, but traffic was beginning to make its way away from the crash site.

Snail's pace? Lightning speed?

She didn't have a clue. All that mattered was Raphael. The sweet taste of his lips. The tang of salt on his skin. The rough bristles of growth upon his cheeks shifting past her fingertips as she swept her hands into a loose cinch behind his neck.

She was half tempted to sling a leg up onto one of his hips when a sharp wolf whistle broke through the thick heat of the afternoon air.

They pulled apart, surprised to find themselves the object of an entire fire crew's attention. More wolf whistles began to ring out from passing cars, along with cheers and cries of, "Good on ya, mate!" and "Nice one, cobber!"

Maggie didn't know whether to shrivel up and die of embarrassment or laugh and scream, *Finally!*

Feigning a demureness she knew she didn't possess, she sought her cue from Raphael.

But instead of withdrawing in horror, Raphael rested his hands on Maggie's hips—protectively, almost—and smiled, tipping his chin toward the firemen and drivers before returning his gaze to her. And that bright twinkle in his blue eyes was alight for the first time in… It had been a while. And a long time coming.

"Do you mind? The attention?" he asked, his gentle accent adding an extra level of sensuality to the question.

She shook her head—no. It was a lot better than being the center of attention because she was the only one who knew how to get grease stains out of work overalls. Better by a mile.

She squinted at the setting sun, the brilliant wash of colour doing its magic behind him. Though she would have happily stayed on the roadside, woven into Raphael's arms, absorbing the full impact of just how incredible it was— how incredible *he* was—practical Maggie kicked into gear.

"We'd probably better hit the road. We're going to be driving all night from the looks of things."

"It's too far, Maggie. Especially having worked

flat-out today. *Non.* Is there not a town nearby where we can stay?"

"What? You mean like in a motel or something?"

OMG! One room or two? One room or two?

Raphael pulled back and examined her, his fingers hooked on her hips with a sense of familiarity that unleashed another thrill of expectation in her heart.

One room. Definitely one room.

That was what his eyes were saying…what his hands were saying. The lips just about to meet hers—

"Maggie!" The police officer who had been coordinating the accident scene—Scott Roland—was jogging towards them, waving something vaguely familiar-looking in his hand. "Don't forget your knickers!"

Flames of embarrassment streaked across Maggie's cheeks.

Why, why, *why* had she used her superhero panties as triage color tags?

Scott slowed to a halt in front of them, eyeing the pair of them with a smirk. "I'm not interrupting anything private, am I?"

"Hardly!"

Maggie scooted out of Raphael's loose hold on her hips and reached out to grab her knickers.

"Not so fast, little lady." Scott's features broadened into an ear-to-ear grin. "I think the press might be interested in hearing about the real-life superhero of today's accident."

"I don't think so. *You're* the real hero and no one's interested in your undershorts!" Maggie ground out, trying again—unsuccessfully—to nab the brightly colored bits of cotton that no one was meant to know about apart from her.

So what if she wore superhero knickers to give herself a little private motivation as she worked her way through the inevitable piles of debris and gunk that had built up at the Louis household in her absence? Her secret little charwoman's outfit. Fit for no eyes other than her own!

"Let's see…" Scott was relishing her discomfort. "What do we have here…?"

From perfect moment to perfectly mortifying…

This was the cringe-worthy material nightmares were made of.

If she could just grab them before Raphael—

"I particularly like these ones, Maggie," Scott

said, holding up her favorite pair—the Wonder
Woman knickers—for one and all to see.

"Stop it!"

"What? Or what about these? Don't you want
the world to know you've got Cat Woman panties? I wouldn't mind a glimpse of you in these,
if you don't mind me saying."

He put his fingers at either end of the black
knickers with sassy cat's eyes on them—one for
each buttock—and tipped them back and forth
like a cat about to pounce.

"*I* do."

Raphael reached out, took the knickers, handed
them back to Maggie and then pulled her close to
him, snugly wrapping an arm around her shoulders.

If swooning was still a thing she would be
doing it. And then crawling beneath her car and
crying fat, hot tears that said, *Why, oh, why can't
I be the cool one? Just once!*

"I'm guessing these are Bat Girl?" Scott pulled
one final pair out of his back pocket.

Raphael held out his hand for the panties and
made a *put 'em here* gesture as Scott held them

out: black, with a bright gold bat embossed on the behind.

Unfazed, Scott gave him a wink. "I suppose you've got the matching Superman boxers, then, big boy?"

Raphael tipped his hand back and forth in a move that said, *Maybe I do, maybe I don't. Super-heroes don't tell.*

If Maggie hadn't thought she was in love before, her affections were cast in stone now.

"Right!" Maggie pulled the car into a huge dusty rectangle that served as a car park. "This is us, I guess."

Her state of mind was the same as Raphael's: one part *Why are we still wearing clothes?* to one part *Are we really ready for the next step*?

The hour-long ride to the motel had seen the sun set and their expectations of what was to come rise.

Now that they were here...

In unison, they looked up at the large neon sign blinking in front of them. With its blood-red lettering and handful of blown-out letters, the level of invitation to come on in and stay the night was questionable.

Big Pe e's Road use & ottleshop

Monster made a noise expressing his doubts from the back seat.

"Do you think they have room service?" Raphael asked.

Maggie laughed, then echoed Raphael's dry tone. "If you're after a hunk of cheese stuck between two bits of bread and an ice-cold stubbie I think you might be all right."

"That's more than I grew up with most days." He shrugged nonchalantly, before remembering Maggie still didn't know that side of his upbringing.

She squinted at him, hands still braced on the steering wheel as if she hadn't entirely decided whether or not she was going to let go. "What are you talking about? Compared to me, you had a *lovely* upbringing."

Something instinctive and fierce rose up in Raphael. From what he could remember, *her* upbringing had been similar to Jean-Luc's. "What do you mean, compared to you?"

Maggie rolled her eyes. "No, no... Nothing bad. Just...no fancy Parisian neighborhood with all the trimmings." She tipped her head toward the back seat. "Shall we give Monster a bit of a stroll?"

Raphael agreed, grateful for the chance to stretch his legs and enjoy the cooler night air.

After a few moments of strolling around Raphael tried again, adding as much of a light-hearted tone to his voice as he could. "What was so bad about your upbringing? If I should have brought my sword to your home, you could have warned me."

Maggie laughed and shook her head. "Honestly, it was nothing like that. My family are goofballs, but they're all very loving. It was more…what the town *wasn't*."

"What do you mean?"

She huffed out a laugh. "Suffice it to say Broken Hill doesn't really throw a patch on Paris. Trust me. You're in for a bit of a shocker tomorrow."

He sucked in a breath. Was she ready for the real Raphael? Warts and all?

He reached across to her and took one of her hands in his, tracing along the lines written into her palm. Before things went any further—and he knew in his heart he wanted them to progress—he owed her this much.

"If you think back," he began softly, his eyes trained on hers, "you never actually came to my house."

Maggie's lips parted in protest, but just as quickly she screwed them into a little moue and thought. "It never really occurred to me…"

Her fingers covered her mouth and she drummed them along her lips for a minute—lips he would do anything to be kissing again.

"We did everything at the Couttard's or around Paris, didn't we?"

He nodded.

"Why was that?" She looked utterly baffled.

"My parents were both…how do you say?… fond of a drink. Or eleven. Do you understand?"

Maggie's eyes widened. "It's not strictly a saying, but I get your drift."

She wasn't judging—just listening. She'd been that way when they'd met. He should have trusted her with this information back then.

The fog cleared in his head. How pointless it had all been! To disguise part of himself from her. Maggie's affection for him wasn't attached to wealth or status or—he looked round the dusty car park outside the motel—to Paris. Paris hadn't been a factor. She'd simply cared for *him*.

"They didn't hurt you, did they?"

Raphael shook his head, no. They hadn't been that bad. Most of the time. The odd cuff to the ear. An arm gripped too tightly. Impossible to fulfill their expectations because they simply weren't happy people.

"They weren't horrible—just poor. And not terribly motivated." He shrugged again. It eased his heart to realize he'd let go of that anger long ago.

"So…how did you and Jean-Luc—?"

"Become friends?" Raphael finished for her. "We met at school. My parents had a small apartment—subsidized housing—in the same neighborhood where the Couttards lived, and at school we were seated in alphabetical order."

"Bouchon and Couttard," Maggie murmured, as if saying the names helped her picture the scene. "And they basically…what? Adopted you?"

Raphael gave a soft smile. The Couttards had opened their hearts and their home to him as if they were his own parents.

"Without the formalities, I suppose you could say they did. Jean-Luc didn't have any brothers or sisters and, as you may remember, both his parents were lawyers so they worked a lot. It was one of the reasons Madame Couttard accepted foreign exchange students."

"Someone for Jean-Luc to hang out with?"

"Yes—precisely. And they had always wanted a large family. The year you came, you had the fortune—or misfortune, depending upon how you look at it—of being lumped in with me. If you remember, that was the year Jean-Luc discovered girls?"

Maggie laughed at the memory. "It was impossible to keep track of them all."

She gave Raphael's hand a squeeze, then gave him a *C'mon buddy, we've just pashed in front of a thousand cars* look.

"I suppose you've figured out by now it was a real hardship being 'lumped' in with you." Her eyes brightened with another thought. "So...when Madame Couttard asked you to do something—"

"If you mean something like *not* kiss the beautiful Australian girl even though it would have made me very happy? Yes. I obeyed. I owed them so much."

"I get it now," Maggie said, nodding as she connected the dots. "I would've done the same thing." A twinkle hit her green eyes. "Even if it left a poor Aussie girl heartbroken that she'd gone all the way to France and hadn't been kissed."

Raphael made a noise to protest, but he could tell from her relaxed demeanor that she wasn't chastising him. The past was in the past.

It was a powerfully healing thought—leaving the past where it was and doing everything he could for his future. And he wanted his future to be with Maggie.

"Well, you know…" His voice dropped an octave. "I didn't fly halfway across the world to stand outside a neon lit motel and talk about the past."

"Oh, no?" Maggie's lips curled into a flirtatious smile as her lids dropped to half-mast over those green eyes of hers. "Why *did* you come?"

"I came for you."

If someone had thrown a lightning bolt straight into her heart it would have had less of an effect.

"Me?"

Raphael nodded. "It's taken me a while to figure it out." He shot her a sheepish look. "Sorry for all the glowering and thunderous looks back in Sydney."

She waved off his concerns, her insides still re-

ANNIE O'NEIL

207

covering from the glitter storm of emotion swirling in her chest. "You were fine. You were just
really..."

"French?" he filled in for her, and they both
laughed.

Raphael took a step closer towards her. The air
grew taut with expectation. With promise.

Monster barked. He wanted his tea.

"What do you say we check in? Get this guy
fed and then...bed?"

*Yes, yes—yes, please. If I don't die of antici-
pation first.*

She nodded as nonchalantly as she could.
"Good idea."

A few minutes later they'd met the owners and
reassessed their dodgy motel as a quirky work
in progress. The owners were a young couple
who offered them the "spa room" before showing them a fenced outdoor area complete with
dog house where Monster could stay the night.

"Alors." Raphael held up the large room key,
a mischievous twinkle in his eye. "Shall we?"

"No time like the present!" Maggie chirped too
loudly, and she grabbed her bag and smiled, just
a little impressed that she could even walk. Her
legs were wobbling like jelly.

The second the door to their room clicked shut behind them all Maggie's nervous energy disappeared.

She barely saw the dated bedcover. The art that looked as though someone's grandmother had won it in a tombola with poor pickings. The lampshades she was certain she'd seen at a car boot sale flanking either side of a queen-sized bed that already seemed too far away even though it couldn't have been more than a few footsteps away.

Raphael clearly felt the same way. He backed her against the door, dropped their overnight bags where they stood and cupped her face with his hands, his lips descending to hers for the most beautifully intimate kiss she'd ever known.

Not five minutes later she realized her entire body had shape-shifted into molten lava.

They'd managed to kick their shoes off, but not much more. Her blouse seemed to have lost a couple of buttons. So had that chambray shirt of Raphael's, she noted with a wicked grin as she gave the sweet spot at the base of his throat an entirely out of character lick.

Each moment in Raphael's arms—touching him, being held by him, caressed by him—was lifting her to another level of sexual revelation. Her body responded to his every touch as if she had never known a man before. And, in his arms, she knew there would never be another.

His fingers slid along her sides as he dropped heated kiss after heated kiss onto her neck. The tips of his fingers dipped in at her waist, eliciting a shiver of response along her belly. Her hands sought his, weaving their fingers together, and as one they turned toward the bed.

"Es-tu sûr?" he murmured, his thumb skimming along one of her cheekbones and shifting a stray strand of hair behind her ear.

"I've never been more certain of anything."

And she meant it. It was as if her whole life had been leading to this point. To Raphael.

When they had checked in to the motel they had giggled like the teenagers they had once been.

All that giddy effervescence was gone now.

In its place was electricity. Fire. The building blocks of desire that had begun to form so long ago leading them to this one erotically charged night of discovery.

Before she could sit on the bed Raphael held her at arm's length, looking at her as a man who'd not drunk water in a hundred days might view a clear running mountain brook.

He wanted her. Knowing that in her heart emboldened Maggie.

Where she had once felt timorous and incredibly body-shy with the two or three other boyfriends she'd had, with Raphael she felt... *beautiful*. Powerful, even. Sensual.

It was surprising, considering just how filthy she must be from the day's hard work.

Which gave her an idea...

"Would you like to take a shower?"

A gleam of heated expectation hit Raphael's eyes. It was a look that said, *Yes.* And, *Why aren't we there already?*

Again he took her hand, and they practically raced to the next room.

Much to their surprise, the bathroom *wasn't* a relic of the previous century. It had been updated into a large wet room, with beautiful earth-tone tiles on one wall, thick slabs of hardwood on the controls wall, a gorgeous cobalt-blue-tiled floor and a huge waterfall shower head. A long olive tree plank held an invitingly pristine pile of thick bath towels.

It was perfect.

"Why wait?" Raphael asked, reaching across to the controls, and then pulling her close to him, still completely clothed, he turned on the water.

Maggie lifted her head to the cascade of water, closed her eyes and let it pour down over her. When she opened her eyes she met Raphael's blue gaze, and in that moment she gave her heart to him completely.

Slowly, assuredly, he undid the remaining buttons of Maggie's blouse, dropping kisses on her bare salty skin as he peeled the cotton away first from her shoulders, then her breasts. Her fingers flew to his hair, clutching thick handfuls of the rich chestnut curls as he took one of her nipples into his mouth, slowly swirling his tongue round and round before sucking and caressing her breast as if time were no factor.

And it wasn't. Not anymore.

All that existed was Raphael.

Her second nipple tightened in anticipation of his kiss. A soft moan vibrated the length of her throat when his lips gained purchase. Her entire body responded—lifting, swelling and aching in feverish suspense, waiting for his touch.

Her knee-length skirt suddenly felt too tight. Her knickers too constricting. Every thread of cotton on Raphael's body was in the way of what she really wanted. Skin to skin contact.

She surprised herself by pushing him back against the wooden wall of the wet room, water still pouring over them, taking each side of his shirt in her hands and tearing it in two.

Raphael laughed.

Shock? Surprise, maybe?

Their eyes met and meshed.

No.

Desire.

Up until this point their movements had been slow, sensuous. Each touch, kiss and caress had carried with it a note of precaution, speaking of a wish to ensure they were pleasing the other.

But now a switch had been flicked.

Now their movements became assured, laden with sexual intent. Down went his jeans. One of them kicked them in a heap to one side. Who knew where his boxers went? Not Maggie. Her skirt hit the far wall. A blink of an eye later her lace-just-in-case knickers were history. And her brassiere…? *What* brassiere?

Raphael pulled her against him and as one they groaned with the pleasure of skin-on-skin connection. Hot. Wet. Insatiable.

They soaped one another with beautifully aromatic body wash, teasing, playing as they did so. Her hands swirled through chest hair. His fingers teased along the soft curves of breasts.

When Raphael parted Maggie's legs with one of his own and trailed his hand up and along Maggie's inner thigh she thought she'd scream with pent-up frustration. When his fingers slipped inside her she did scream. Her thighs instinctively clamped tight onto his hand as she begged him to stop. She wanted to reach her peak with him inside her. She wanted to share the exaltation of that ultimate intimacy as one united soul.

A moment later he took her hand in his and filled it with shower gel, lifting his eyebrows, taunting her to have as wicked a way with him as she could imagine.

Maggie didn't have to imagine. Having the real Raphael here and now was all the inspiration she needed.

Bathed in soft light, warm water and the gentle gaze of the man she loved, Maggie enjoyed the slick sensation of shifting a soapy hip along one of Raphael's solid thighs, her soft belly against his well-defined stomach, then moving lower... to the hard, taut, evidence of his desire.

The temptation to wrap her hands round his neck, lift her legs to his hips and lower herself onto the solid, velvety thickness of his erection nearly blinded her to any other option.

The scenario played itself out as they moved from the drenched wall behind them to the beautiful rich blue tiles beneath their feet. The need for protection shifted the immediacy of her desire into the tantalizing prospect of toweling him off and starting all over again on the bed.

As if reading her mind, Raphael turned off the water and reached for the pile of thick bath towels. He unfurled one of the towels, wrapped her in it, and swiftly secured one around his own trim hips.

Just two seconds of being hidden from him and already Maggie felt deprived of all six foot two inches of Raphael's beautifully toned body.

Depraved, more like.

But not indecently so. More as if she'd found the key to a special door—*une porte magique*. A portal that gave her access to the richness of carnal desire with someone who was safe, someone who cared, someone who loved her as much as she loved him.

A few long-strided steps later and Raphael was ripping the covers off the bed. He was right. They didn't need anything to hide from each other.

She ran towards the bed and launched herself at it, laughing with sheer delight.

Raphael turned back from his overnight bag and held up an easily recognizable foil packet.

"You came prepared?" She feigned shock.

"I came with hope," he parried, a naughty choirboy expression playing across his features.

"Good answer." She crooked her finger and beckoned for him to join her.

Once he'd stretched out to his full length on the bed and begun reaching for her she shook that finger—no.

Plucking the packet from his hand, she straddled him, saying, "Now it's my turn to drive *you* wild."

Raphael was astonished at Maggie's transformation.

Temptress. Tactician. *Femme fatale*. All wrapped into one flame-haired package of feminine beauty.

She smiled above him, her feline eyes weighted with desire as she lowered herself just enough to give him luxurious kiss after luxurious kiss. Then, slowly, she began to work her way down.

Her lips grazed his nipples, her tongue darting out for hot, quick licks as she ran her fingers along his chest as if it were clay she was about to mold into a thing of beauty.

"You're beautiful," he whispered.

"You're all I've ever wanted." She lifted herself so that her lips shifted across his own as she spoke.

"Je t'aime."

Maggie's eyes glassed over and a single tear dropped onto his cheek.

"Je t'aime aussi."

He loved her.

At long last he'd found her, and he would never let her go.

Maggie shifted so that she was straddling one of his legs.

She looked like a goddess. Her damp hair tumbled down in waves and curls along her shoulders. Little drips of water were wending their careless way along the curves and dips of her breasts. When he tried to reach out and touch them she tsked at him and wagged a finger—no.

She lifted up the condom and smiled.

It was time.

Mieux vaut tard que jamais.

He might be thirteen years too late for the kiss he should've given her as a teen, but something told him the timing was exactly right for making love to this woman he'd always held in his heart.

Maggie's hands shook as she unwrapped the small packet. When she touched him, he met her hands with his own, helping her guide the protection along the length of his erection.

And then he couldn't wait anymore.

"*Maintenant.*"

"Now?" She smiled, lifting herself up from his leg as she did.

"*Oui. Mais doucement.*"

Taunt me. That was what he was saying. Fast. Slow. She could do what she wanted, but he needed to be inside her. *Now.*

Teasingly at first, hinting at the warm depths that would surround him, she lowered herself in excruciatingly slow increments, occasionally raising herself up again so that the cool night air hit him, until he couldn't bear it anymore.

He placed his hands on her hips and teased her

down the length of him until she covered him completely. Together they moaned as she began to rock her hips back and forth, back and forth, until he thought he would go mad. Pressing his fingertips onto her hips, he encouraged her to set herself free. To abandon herself to the desire they felt for each other.

He lifted his hips, pressed them towards her with a drive and desire he'd never known before. Again and again their bodies met and sparked, sending waves of pleasure through him in such heated blasts that he couldn't restrain his longing for her anymore.

"Be with me!" he cried, his eyes connecting with hers more powerfully than they had ever done before.

It was impossible to tell if she'd heard him or not. Maggie glowed with exertion and desire.

He lifted himself up, wrapped an arm around her waist and flipped her over so that he was on top.

Her smile spoke volumes. *Take me,* it said. *I'm all yours.*

He thrust into her with renewed vigor. Hips meeting hips. Maggie's legs wrapping around him and pulling him in closer. Her thighs, breasts, belly—every touch was hypnotic and energizing. When her fingernails dug into his shoulders and scored the length of his back he knew he couldn't hold back any longer.

He met her green eyes and as if by mutual agreement they allowed themselves the luxury of the ultimate mutual release.

The detonation of pleasure was initially so powerful that he couldn't even see.

Pulling her close to him, he rolled to one side, still inside her, feeling their breath intermingling as they each floated back to earth.

"Well, that was nice," Maggie said eventually, her full grin making it obvious she had just made the understatement of the year.

"Comme-ci, comme-ca."

He played along, tipping his hand back and forth between them, letting it come to a rest atop her rapidly beating heart. He placed her free hand on his own chest, proof that his heart was pounding in time with hers.

They both knew there was nothing so-so about what had just happened between them.

They lay together in silence, wrapped in one

another's arms. Gathering their breath, their thoughts, enjoying the simple pleasure of gazing into each other's eyes until eventually Maggie asked, "Do you fancy room service?" before dissolving into another fit of giggles.

CHAPTER NINE

"WELCOME TO BROKEN HILL!"

Maggie used her best tour guide voice, hoping the anxiety building in her chest wasn't bleeding through.

The morning had been magical. Of course. How could it not have been when she'd woken up to sweet kisses being dropped onto her lips by Raphael as he held her close to him?

Leaving the motel room had proved tough, so they'd opted for a late check-out and made the most of it.

Eventually—reluctantly—Maggie had answered her brothers' building number of texts and said they'd be there by teatime.

The closer they got to home, the harder the Cinderella syndrome struck.

Cinderella the morning after the ball.

The further away from the roadhouse they drove, the less she believed it had really happened.

No glass slippers anywhere. Just a girl and a guy in a car on the way to her childhood madhouse.

Raphael had gone very quiet over the last few hours of their journey. Rather than ask him what he was thinking, she had let the all too familiar fingers of doubt begin niggling away at her confidence.

Did he regret telling her he loved her?

Was making love to her and meeting her family in a twenty-four-hour period too much, too soon?

Perhaps the whole thing had simply been a release after the accident.

He'd never attended a huge pile-up like that. And it had to have unleashed some pretty dark memories.

He'd told her he *loved* her. That wasn't something that just slipped out.

"It's not as big as I expected," Raphael said as the town came into view.

His tone was hard to read—not a hint of anything other than general surprise in his voice. No disdain. No, *Have mercy upon me—I just had sex with a girl from the Woop Woop.*

Not yet, anyway.

"Well, you're probably going to see a lot of

things you didn't expect over the next couple of days."

She offered him an apologetic smile, then returned her gaze to the road, chiding herself as she did.

Just because she'd entered the town's limits it didn't mean she was submitting herself to a life of servitude. All she'd have to do was unearth the kitchen counters from who knew how many weeks of washing up, scrub the floors, air the place…

Raphael would understand if she had to do fifteen loads of laundry before they headed back to Sydney, right?

To buy a bit more time she took "the scenic route", pointing out an enormous red bench someone had built eons earlier near one of the old mine sites.

"What is it for?" Raphael asked.

It was a reasonable question, considering there wasn't really anything else near it. It was just a giant bench in the middle of the desert.

"No idea," she admitted. "Aussies like big things. If you had enough time on your hands you could visit them all. The country is full of them. A ginormous banana, a guitar, a sundial…"

She forced herself to stop, surprised at how long she could have prattled on. As if her country's super-sized objects were part of her. Which, of course, they weren't. But the culture was—the landscape, the air. They were *all* part of who she was. Who she would become.

Would Raphael stay and become a part of that too?

He peered out of the window and made one of those French noises that meant, *Peculiar, but I like it*.

It made her smile. But it made her a little sad, too. This was probably the first and last time he'd ever be here.

"We used to come out here all the time. To see the bench."

Why she'd loved it so much was beyond her. But she had begged her parents and her brothers to help her clamber up onto it countless times. They'd done so gladly, climbing up themselves after they'd hoisted her up, and then they'd all sat and watched the world go by—excepting the time a dust storm had blown in and they'd high-tailed it home so her mother's asthma didn't kick up.

Little had they known her coughing was actually lung cancer.

Raphael refocused his gaze on her, his smile shifting into a concerned frown. "Are you happy to be home?"

Maggie shot Raphael a quick smile she knew looked more nervous than chirpy.

Excited?

Not really.

Nervous?

Completely.

"Sure..." she said finally.

It wasn't much of an answer, but it would have to do. Although hightailing it back to Sydney had a certain appeal. There was so much she still hadn't told Raphael—so many reasons he might begin to regret last night.

She bit down on her lower lip and trapped it tight.

Why was coming home so painful?

It didn't take a surgeon—or indeed a paramedic—to figure that one out.

Coming home reminded her of all the dreams she hadn't realized. And having Raphael next to her was a double reminder. *He'd* gone and done it—he'd fulfilled those teenage dreams of becoming a surgeon.

She glanced at her road trip companion, unsurprised to see him looking bemused as they passed the mismatched series of houses that made up Broken Hill's eclectic aesthetic.

Wood. Cinderblock. Corrugated metal sheets rusted the same color as the iron-red earth they sat upon—and, of course, the centerpieces of the ever-shrinking town's main street: two traditionally built brick and stone hotels. Glorious yesteryear structures that sang of a golden era when precious metals had all but sprung from the earth.

Now the town was doing its best to reinvent itself as a tourist destination, but with water in short supply and not much to do if you weren't into collecting Outback art or looking at solar panels...

The place was about as far a cry from Paris as you could get, short of a village made of igloos.

Sitting at a traffic light, Maggie stared at the grand old structures. When she was little she'd thought they were the most beautiful buildings she'd ever seen. When she'd returned from Paris...well, a lot of things had changed after she'd returned from Paris.

Maggie's knuckles emptied of blood, her grip tightening on the steering wheel as she drove on a few more minutes and eventually pulled the car into the familiar covered carport.

It had been haphazardly tacked onto the family property years ago, when her brothers had flirted with the idea of becoming construction workers before finally settling upon becoming auto mechanics and setting up their own garage. The fact the carport roof was listing indicated they'd chosen wisely.

There were few signs of life in front of the wooden house, but that wasn't unusual. With their house situated only a couple of streets away from the main street, her brothers often shifted from their auto repair business to the hotel a couple of doors down for a few drinks—and, she imagined, since she was no longer there to cook for them, some dinner.

She stared at the entryway to the house, surprised to see that the trim had been repainted from a mysterious orange to a rich blue that matched the sky. In fact the whole house had been repainted.

The façade of the four-bedroom bungalow had been peeling under the desert-strength heat of the Australian sun for as long as she could remember.

So what?

A paint job didn't mean anything. It was just the same thing as if she'd taken herself out for a manicure. Superficial changes—nothing more. Hardly proof her family had changed after all these years. She stared down at her unpainted nails.

"Are you all right?"

"Yeah, sure." Maggie smiled at Raphael, almost surprised to see him there. He looked so out of context here. "Just…adjusting."

She made a fuss over tidying up a couple of serviettes left over from their trip and finishing off her water as Raphael unclipped Monster's harness and put him on a lead.

She squinted against the afternoon sun as the pair of them walked toward the house, with Monster bimbling around, sniffing this and that, as Raphael soaked in the atmosphere.

Would he stay in Australia? Make Monster a permanent part of his life? Make *her* a permanent part of his life?

She pulled her fingers through her hair and teased it into a loose plait. This wasn't the time to be asking herself questions like that.

"Maggie?" Raphael gave her a questioning look. *"C'est ta maison, n'est-ce pas?"*

"Oui, oui." Maggie confirmed on automatic pilot, then checked herself.

This wasn't Paris. Or Sydney. This was the Woop Woop and the only way to fit in was to go back to being the girl who hadn't known the difference between the Louvre and the loo.

"Prepare yourself," she said to Raphael.

"For what?"

The meaty revving of a quad bike drowned out anything she was about to say, followed by some very familiar whoops and hollers. She rolled her eyes. Sounded like another Louis Brothers experiment.

"You'll see."

Very little could have prepared Raphael for the scene unfolding in front of them as they walked through the carport and around to the back of Maggie's childhood home. Instead of the postage-stamp-sized garden he had been expecting there was a huge open sprawl of land that at one point might have been destined for another row of houses.

Two men were on the back of an all-terrain vehicle, pulling something attached to two enormous elastic bands which were, in turn, attached to two unused telephone poles. Just off to the left another man was holding up a video camera, feet propped on an Esky, a broad smile on his face.

Only when the men on the ATV released the "object" did Raphael realize it was another man. As he flew through the air and bounced back and forth against the rubbery pull of the super-sized slingshot the group collectively dissolved into fits of hysterical laughter and self-congratulation.

So this was Maggie's family.

"I told you Aussies like big toys," Maggie said dryly, her eyes rolling as if this was an everyday sight in the Louis backyard. She put a hand to the side of her mouth and called above the roar of laughter, "Get Dad down from there, you lot! Are you trying to get yourselves a Darwin Award? No prizes for proving you are idiots by vaulting father into the strastophere!"

"Daggie!" As one, the two men on the ATV turned around, leapt off the vehicle, ran to Maggie and picked her up and squished her into a big brother sandwich.

Une baguette de Maggie, Raphael thought, a smile hitting his face as Maggie laughed and protested in equal turns. Her protests gathered strength when the other two men joined them and followed suit with a second, more rigorous hug and a proper knuckleduster.

This boisterous homecoming was a far cry from anything he could have expected. A hit of emotion gripped his heart and squeezed. It wasn't envy he was feeling... *Longing.* That was what it was. Longing to be part of a family. The sensation hit him hard.

She was part of a family. He didn't have anyone to offer her. Two years ago he would've had the Couttards...

"Let me down, you oafs!" Maggie finally shouted.

"Where's your girlfriend, Dags?"

"I didn't bring a girlfriend." She looked across at Raphael. "I brought...um... I brought Raphael."

The men—all tall, strongly built alpha males—turned to him with narrowed eyes and flexing hands. Maggie looked like a china doll next to the four of them. A china doll with a killer left hook.

"But..." One of the men shot her a bewildered look. "He's a *bloke.*"

"Yeah, glad you figured that one out on your lonesome." Maggie's expression was decidedly... *mixed.* Annoyed. Embarrassed. Hopeful. Anxious.

"But..." One of the other brothers took a step

forward. "You didn't say anything about bringing a *bloke*."

"I didn't say anything about bringing a girlfriend either. What does it matter?"

Hmm… Not a straightforward case of "meet my new lover", then.

"Well, it doesn't, Dags." The final brother stepped even closer and said, "Except…"

"Except what?" Maggie snapped back. "Except you've forgotten your manners and how to say, *G'day, nice to meet you, Raphael. Can I offer you a cold drink after your long journey?*"

"We've got plans tonight."

"So? We include him in them. What's the big deal?" Maggie glanced across at Raphael and gave him a *See? I told you they were a pain* look.

"Who are you, anyway?" asked the younger brother, lifting his chin as he gave Raphael a sidelong glare then moved his eyes to his sister. "We thought you were bringing one of your girlie friends from the big city to show her how real Australians get on."

Raphael was certain he saw the man's biceps twitch in anticipation.

"Raphael is…" She drew out the word, obviously struggling to find the best way to describe him.

There were a number of options she could choose from.

Colleague?

Friend with benefits?

Love of her life who couldn't make any promises?

"Raphael. Dr. Raphael Bouchon. He's testing the waters over here in Oz for a bit. We're on an ambo together. He was sort of my host-brother-type-of-thing when I lived in France." She shot him another apologetic smile.

Or that.

Her description stung. But what else was she meant to say?

He hadn't even told her whether he was staying in Australia.

He didn't know himself.

The part of him that knew he loved Maggie wanted to.

The other part—the part that couldn't keep at bay the memories of the day Jean-Luc had told him to leave his family's home, that all he did was take—that part still wasn't at peace with his past.

"Well, then, welcome, Frenchie." One of her brothers kept his gaze solidly on Raphael as he spoke. "So, Dags…what sort of sleeping arrangements are you after for your friend?"

All eyes turned to Raphael.

Though the sun had long passed over the yard-arm, it still burnt down on them with a fierceness completely unlike the summer heat in Sydney. Or perhaps it was the family's heated glares that had Raphael pulling himself up to his full height.

With their Wild West demeanor, he would not have been the tiniest bit surprised to see each of the Louis men shift aside their jackets—if they'd been wearing them—to reveal sheriff's badges and holstered pistols in preparation for running him out of town if he so much as suggested he would very much approve of sharing a bed with Maggie.

It looked as if he was back to being a teenager. Looked as if he was back to being judged.

"For heaven's sake, Ed." Maggie punched one brother in the arm. "Could you not call me that anymore?"

The tension lessened as Ed relaxed his pistols-at-dawn pose and looked at the rest of his family and Raphael in disbelief. "What's this I hear? My kid sister doesn't like being the Dagster anymore? What's wrong with being our little Digga-dagga-doo?"

He cooed and gave her a little tickle under the chin, all the while calling her Dags. Whatever that was.

"I know this might sound completely mental to you lot..." Maggie crossed her arms defensively over her chest, a smile twitching at the corner of her lips "...but now that I'm a big girl, I think I might actually like to be called by my *real* name in front of our guest." She ground out the last part of her sentence and flicked her eyes in Raphael's direction.

"Oh, I doooo beg your pahhhdon." Ed put on a faux, hoity-toity English accent and bowed. "Did you bring *royalty* from the big city, Princess Margaret?"

Ed received another punch from his sister without so much as a blink.

Through gritted teeth Maggie turned and grimaced. "Raphael, I have the very obvious *dis*pleasure of introducing you to my feral family. Boys, this is Raphael. He was my best friend when I was in Paris and is a proper badass on the ambo. Not to mention a surgeon who is completely capable of removing all of your internal organs. Come along, then. Line up."

She clapped her hands together and in a well-practiced maneuver they lined up alongside her.

"This is my father, Joseph."

"Any friend of Maggie's is welcome here, mate." Her father reached forward to give Raphael a bone-crushing handshake before giving him a quick wink. "And Daddo or Joe'll do just fine."

"This is Edward," Maggie continued, pretending not to listen to the correction.

"Eddie, Ed or Big Fella work for me."

Raphael braced himself for another über-macho handshake, only to receive an abbreviated military salute instead, followed by a display of dark-stained hands the size of pie pans.

"Sorry, mate. My mitts are covered in grease. Wouldn't want to get your city slicker clothes all mucky straight off the bat, would we?"

Maggie gave an exasperated sigh and quickly introduced her other two brothers—Nate and Billy—both of whom seemed to be quite happy to be called Nate and Billy and to shake hands with Raphael in a straightforward, if slightly suspicious fashion.

"You made good time from—where was it you stayed last night?" asked Billy.

Maggie flushed bright red and muttered something about the roadhouse and the accident scene.

Billy nodded, clocking his sister's pinkening cheeks, then cocked his head to the side and crossed his arms over his gym-toned chest. He looked as if he was deciding whether or not to give Raphael a black eye.

Raphael pressed his heels into the ground. He'd take a shiner for Maggie. It was the least he could do, considering he had no answers to give her about a future together.

"Be honest with me, mate," Billy began, "did Daggie tell you we were a bunch of half-witted losers or did we get better billing?"

Raphael looked to Maggie, hoping for some sort of cue on how to respond to the question. Another eye-roll answered his raised brows.

"What is a Daggie?" he asked instead.

Her brothers fell about laughing so hard they were near enough swiping tears from their eyes.

"Please." Maggie drew in a deep breath and shook her head. "Do not pay attention to the cave people in my life. A 'dag', if you must know, is an Aussie term for a person who is a bit…" Her green eyes flicked up to the sky as she sought the right definition. "Someone who is a bit like we were in high school."

"She's trying to say an A-Grade nerd," Nate jumped in, giving his sister another friendly knuckleduster.

"Aw, mate! So you were a *nerd*?" Billy's friendliness shot up a notch. "Got it. One of the book squad. Makes sense."

Maggie flushed a bit. "No, boys. *I* was a nerd. But Raphael...he was..." For an infinitesimal moment their eyes caught and then her brothers started gabbling away again.

What had she been about to say? The flush on her cheeks suggested she was glad she hadn't said it. The cinch in his heart wished she had.

"Who's this little creature, eh?" Ed knelt down and called Monster to him.

Raphael unclipped the lead, surprised to see Monster run to Ed, tail wagging, virtually jumping up and down with anticipation of getting scratched behind the ears.

"His name's Monster. He's looking for a home."

Ed sent him a sharp look. "What? This little guy's not yours? What'd you do? Kidnap him?"

"He adopted Raphael back in Sydney," Maggie jumped in giving Raphael a curious look.

Monster lay on his back and wiggled his paws in the air, easily wooing Ed into giving his furry belly a good old scrub.

The dog was obviously drawn to him. And Raphael couldn't blame him. By all appearances Ed was a settled, happy, solid guy. A man content with life and his place in it.

The type of man *he* needed to be before he took the next step in loving Maggie. And he wanted to take that step. But with one foot still firmly cemented in the past he didn't know how.

"It looks like Monster's affections have changed…" Raphael lifted up his hands, as if to add, *He's yours if you want him*, but instantly he felt the loss of his little four-legged companion.

Now it was Maggie's turn to shoot daggers at him.

He swallowed.

What was he *doing*? Giving away Monster was akin to saying *au revoir* to Maggie in the crudest way possible. Bidding her farewell by proxy.

"Hey, Mags…" Nate sidled over to his sister's side and gave her a poke in the ribs. "I don't know if Frenchie is going to like our plans for dinner."

"Why?" Maggie shot an alarmed look between her brothers, then leveled her gaze at her father. "Dad…what have you let these larrikins dream up? Wait a minute!" She held up her hands, her jaw dropping. "You're not actually telling me you've made dinner all by yourselves."

They all laughed uproariously.

Raphael guessed that was a "no" on the home-made supper, then.

Maggie's father smiled mischievously and stroked his stubbled chin. "I think I'd better let your brothers explain about your birthday pressie."

"Birthday?" Raphael sent her a questioning look. "You didn't say it was your birthday."

Ed, or maybe it was Billy, slung a congenial arm across his shoulder. "She's a sly one, our Dags. Doesn't say half of what goes on in that big ol' brain of hers. That's why we thought she deserved a bit of TLC from her big brothers."

"What? TLC in the form of letting me clean your house, do your laundry and make my own cake?" Maggie's hands flew to her hips and an indignant expression that ought to have elicited steam from her ears hit her face. "Yeah. You guys *really* know how to treat a girl."

Nate guffawed. "Laundry's all done, Mags. All you have to do is get yourself scrubbed up for a night on the town. And..." he flicked a thumb at Raphael "...your mate here can tag along if he wants, but I don't know if it'll really float his *bateau.*"

Raphael smiled. Not as much of a country bumpkin as he let on, then. He'd have to be careful. He'd have to win her brothers over. Without their approval he didn't stand a chance.

Maggie eyed the lot of them skeptically. The lot of her family, that was. Her eyes failed to connect with Raphael's.

If he'd known it was her birthday...

He would've what? Bought her a diamond ring and asked her to marry him?

"What have you boys planned?" Maggie's eyes crackled with impatience.

Some of that ire had to have been fuelled by him. Surprise parties were usually met with a smile.

"It's a secret," Billy said, tapping the side of his nose and then giving his sister a scan. "Got anything a bit more girlie than what you're wearing right now?"

Maggie's lids lowered as she evil-eyed her

brothers, who collectively started kicking at the dirt and looking at the sky as if they weren't hearing a word of the conversation.

"Again, I ask you. *What* have you planned?"

"Perhaps you should head on down to the hotel and get changed. For tonight."

"Hotel? What happened to my room?"

"Aw, yeah...about that."

"Yeah, *that*."

Maggie's heart was thumping so hard in her chest she wouldn't have been surprised if it had started ricocheting around under her blouse. What on earth was going on? This morning Raphael had been the picture of an adoring...what? Boyfriend? Lover? And now that he'd met her family he was giving them his dog and looking as if he'd rather be anywhere but here.

Terrific.

Just as she'd predicted. Who would want to take on a family as mad as hers?

No one. That was who.

And, to make matters worse, she didn't even have her childhood bed to throw herself on and sob away her loss.

"It's been a while since you've lived here, Mags..." Nate scrubbed his hands through his short strawberry-blond hair. "We reckoned you weren't coming back so we sort of made it into a storeroom."

A level of hurt she hadn't expected to feel filled her gut.

"A storeroom?"

"Yeah. You know—extra parts for cars and suchlike. Billy put in some shelves. It looks good." There was a note of apology in his voice, but not enough to say, *Welcome home, sis.*

Maggie knew she didn't have the right to protest. She'd been gone a long time. Years. And had given no indication that she would ever be moving back.

"Don't pull a face like that, Mags. As I said, there's no need to throw your swag blanket under the stars or anything. We got you a room at the hotel."

Ed picked up the "no worries" mantle and gave a carefree shrug. "Ralph can stay here."

"Raphael," she ground out. "It's Raphael." Her eyes widened. "Wait. Why would he stay here?"

"Well, there was only one room left at the hotel." Her brother gave her a no-brainer face. "And that's yours."

"Yeah, well, I—"

I'd rather stay with Raphael?

She shot him a *Help me out, here,* look, not a little worried about his response. Or lack of one. Was he going to stand up for her, as he had with the knickers and the policeman at the crash site? Throw an arm around her shoulder with a she's-with-me attitude emanating from his every pore?

A hit of regret that she hadn't put on her Super Girl knickers that morning jagged through her. This morning she'd felt so *sure*! So certain of herself. Of Raphael.

Before she had a moment to process the expression developing on Raphael's face Billy was elbowing past Ed while pulling something out of his back pocket.

He presented her with a pink envelope with tiny little strawberries laced around the edges. All of the breath left Maggie's lungs in an instant. When she saw her name written in her mother's delicate script tears blurred her vision.

"Here, Mags. We found this when we cleaned out your room."

"What is it?"

He shrugged and stared at it, as if seeing it for the first time. "Well, I dunno, do I? It's addressed to you. We found it behind your headboard." His voice turned a bit gruff as he continued, "Mum must've put it under your pillow, or something, before she—you know. She must've left it for you."

He held the envelope out and shook it in a gesture for her to take it. With trembling fingers she reached out, took the envelope in her hand and pressed it to her heart.

"Right." Billy clapped his hands together and shook the obvious swell of memories from his expression. "Since no one seems particularly keen on changing into their fancy duds, whaddya think about heading into town and getting this show on the road?"

CHAPTER TEN

AFTER AGREEING TO leave Monster at the family home while they headed into town, Raphael and Maggie climbed into the car. As he clicked the door shut Raphael felt the confines of the vehicle make Maggie's mood significantly more pronounced.

Whether it was the unopened letter, his insensitive behavior, her brothers or all three was difficult to divine. The least he could do was start setting the record straight in *his* corner. He did love her. He did want her. But he needed to put some things right in his own house before he could offer her full access to his heart.

The wheels screeched as she turned a corner.

"Thank you for inviting me here. It's wonderful to see where you grew up and meet your family."

"Well, it's not over yet," Maggie grumbled, her eyes flicking to her rearview mirror to see where her brothers were following in a Louis men convoy.

"Your family seem to love you very much," he tried.

"If treating me like a twelve-year-old virgin is the definition of *love* then—" She stopped herself. "Well, yeah, they do love me, but…" Her tone suggested familial love wasn't the problem.

If only she knew what it felt like to have the people you loved most—the people you saw as family—withdraw their affections, she would understand what he was going through. But until he had it completely figured out he didn't want to muddle things more than he already had, so he lumbered ahead, trying to make a light joke of things.

"You don't like surprises?"

The look on her face indicated that he shouldn't be looking to start a career in stand-up comedy anytime soon.

"Not when I've just opened my heart to someone and they go and offer to give their bloody dog away because they don't even know if they're sticking around, I don't," she snapped.

"I shouldn't have done that. With Monster…" he admitted. "And nothing's set in stone."

"So." She clapped a hand against the center component of the steering wheel. "What exactly does this mean? Will you be coming back to Sydney with me or will you be flying back to Paris straight out of Broken Hill?"

"You can *do* that?"

The second the words left his mouth he knew it was the worst thing he could have said. And the one thing he needed to do.

The ominous mood around Maggie grew and multiplied until it all but developed into a force field around her.

"Maggie, please."

"Maggie, please…what?"

Maggie's emotion was barely contained. Her eyes were glassed with obvious frustration as her foot became a bit heavier on the pedal. Not exactly the ideal mood for driving.

"Please pull over the car. Let's talk about this."

"We're here anyway," she snapped, abruptly yanking the car into a space in front of one of the traditional hotels that dominated the main street.

"Maggie—" Raphael reached out to touch her arm and she pulled it away.

"Don't." She turned in her seat to face him. "Don't do that if all you want to do is to leave. I've missed enough in my life because of you!"

She covered her mouth and gasped, tears immediately cascading down her cheeks.

"I'm sorry," she sobbed. "I shouldn't have said that. It wasn't your fault. That was a horrible thing to say. It wasn't your fault at all."

"*What* wasn't?"

The over-familiar sensation of dread—of guilt—began creeping into his bloodstream.

"Missing my mum. Not seeing her before she died."

A buzzing began in his ears as he struggled to make the connections. Maggie had never told him the whole story. Though she rarely alluded to it, he knew her mother was no longer alive, but he hadn't pressed, well aware that his own ghosts were hard enough to contain without forcing someone else to release theirs.

He pulled a fresh handkerchief from his pocket and handed it to her. It was one of the few lessons he'd learned from his own mother before she'd succumbed to the temptations of drink—*"Il ne faut rien laisser au hazard,"* she would say, pressing a single, freshly ironed square of cloth into his hand each morning.

Leave nothing to chance.

It had been their one moment of true connection each day. The last thing she'd said to him before she'd passed away. And Maggie had missed that own moment with her mother.

Leave nothing to chance.

The words lodged in his heart.

They spoke of action. Risk.

Was opening his heart to more rejection a risk he was prepared to take?

Maggie steadied her breath and began to speak. "We'd planned… Well… I'd been dreaming of a trip to France ever since I read *Beauty and the Beast* when I was little."

She went on to detail how she and her mother had planned the trip in meticulous detail. How her mother had been secretly scrimping and saving ever since they'd first read the fairy tale and Maggie had become transfixed. A dreamy-eyed country girl going to the most magical place in the world…

"Going to Paris was a dream come true."

"And your mother? What happened while you were away?"

Maggie swiped a few more tears away and sniffed, unable to meet his eyes. "I didn't know it, but she had lung cancer."

Conflicting emotions threatened to split him in two.

Half of him ached to reach out and touch her, hold her in his arms and tell her how sorry he was for her loss. The other half respected the determined look on Maggie's face, her need to tell the story once and never again. He nodded for her to continue. He'd hear her out and then he'd leave. He'd face his own demons head-on, as she was doing here in Broken Hill.

"She was pretty far along when I left, but we all thought it was something else. Something curable. She told us her cough was asthma-related." Anguish filled her voice as she continued, "We didn't *know*! *I* didn't know. My brothers eventually made her tell them the truth, and she started to get treatment while I was away, but she swore them to secrecy."

A sob escaped her throat.

"She told them they weren't to do or say anything that would interrupt my year. I finally figured it out the day I was flying home."

"How?"

"She hadn't come to the phone in over a fortnight. She'd sent emails and little notes, but her handwriting had changed. Had become weak and scratchy. When she wouldn't come to the phone to wish me a good flight I finally demanded that my brothers tell me. I wasn't getting on that plane until I knew what was going on. They said she'd just been admitted to the local hospice."

Her green eyes shone with streams of tears but her voice sounded dull when she finally spoke.

"I presume I don't need to spell out why she was there."

He shook his head, no, grateful that her mother had been given appropriate palliative care. He was astonished at the strength of a mother's love.

"That plane couldn't move fast enough," Maggie said. "It was the longest journey of my life."

"And when you arrived?" He already knew the answer, but he had to hear it from her.

"She passed away three hours before I got here." Maggie stared at him, strangely dry-eyed, as if something inside her had died all over again. "My brothers and my father had been with her the whole time. I was the only one who wasn't there for the one person who had sacrificed so much for me to reach my dreams."

A sharp series of knocks sounded on the side of the car.

"Dags! Let's get a move on. Time to celebrate, birthday girl!"

Maggie swooshed her sleeve across her eyes and rolled down her window with a huff. "Quit rushing me, you big drongo."

She gave her hair a bit of a princess shake and shooed her brother away with her fingers. A lit-tle-sister-in-charge-of-her-big-brother move that would have made him laugh if Raphael hadn't known she was hurting so much inside.

"It's my birthday, I'll come in when I'm ready."

"You all right, Maggie?"

Raphael clocked Eddie's use of his sister's real name. Genuine concern. Family love.

"Yeah. Fine. Just…you know…getting myself prepared to enter the hotel after who knows how long. I'll be there in a minute."

"Raph? Are you not coming in to celebrate Maggie's big three-oh?"

This one was up to Maggie. He wasn't going to prolong the torture if she didn't want him there.

"I don't know." She looked across at him, with nothing but questions and defiance written across her features. "*Are* you coming in?"

This wasn't a win-win situation. It was lose all the way. But leaving was the coward's option and he didn't want to be *that* guy anymore. The one who walked away when the going got tough.

Don't leave anything to chance.

This time he'd see it through.

"Of course, Maggie."

She held out the handkerchief towards him, then pulled it back. "I'll wash it first."

"Keep it." He gave her hand a squeeze, doing his best to ignore the flinch that followed in its wake. "I want you to have it."

"Terrific." She gave the handkerchief a wry smile, and as her brother opened the car door for her she muttered, "Something to remind me of the best and worst birthday I've ever had."

"Why are we going in the back way? Where's Dad? You haven't put him in your slingshot to get him here, have you?"

Maggie knew she was being irritable because things were being yanked out of her control again now that she was back home.

Little sister mode.

Doing what she was told.

Correction.

Doing what was expected of her.

Which was following in her nutty big brothers'

wake and then, most likely, cleaning up the inevitable mess.

Despite her determination to stay grouchy, her heart softened as she followed her brothers into the hotel. There were the usual shout-outs to the lads, all of whom played locally for an Aussie Rules footie team. Of course. The "When in the blue blazes are you going to get my car fixed?" questions were followed by a friendly laugh and a promise to buy them a drink if they went to the bar.

And there were a few other comments Maggie didn't quite understand.

"When do you want us to have the bits and pieces in place?"

"Are you sure you got the right music?"

And, the most disconcerting of all, "I've told the wife to bring her camera. This is going to be legendary."

That one she *couldn't* let go.

She skipped-ran to catch up to Nate, aiming for casual but landing on high-pitched panic. "Nate, my dear big brother, if this is some strange thing like being hit by thirty cream pies in front of the whole of Broken Hill, I am *out*."

Raphael caught up with them, but met no one's

eye. He had reverted straight back to being the brooding, mysteriously enigmatic man who had met her at the Sydney Botanical Gardens all those weeks ago. The one she wasn't entirely sure she knew anymore.

Well, now she knew a lot more than she'd bargained for.

Yes, he was an incredible doctor. And he had suffered a deep loss. It seemed to have made a permanent mark on him—one that wouldn't allow full access to his heart. Unless he was able to forgive himself...

She tried to swallow the frustration building in her throat.

Why hadn't she been enough?

This was buyer's remorse at its cruelest.

He might have made sweet, intimate love to her. He might have whispered his innermost feelings. But there hadn't been any promises. Only some ridiculously unsubtle back-pedaling the second he'd got an eyeful of the real Maggie Louis.

Just what a girl needed on her thirtieth. Not that she'd forewarned him of that. Becoming an official spinster was traumatizing enough. She'd thought she'd cracked it on the eve of her birthday... Cinderella Syndrome, indeed. Only this time the handsome Prince had figured out that Cinders wasn't really all that and was going to hightail it back to his castle. Sooner rather than later if the expression on his face was anything to go by.

"All right, Mags." Billy turned around when they reached one of the lounges that were usually used for private parties. "Can you just wait here with Raphael for a minute?"

She nodded.

Billy threw a couple of looks between the pair of them, then leaned in and whispered, "He's not the jealous type, right? You're just mates?"

Less than twelve hours ago she knew her smile would have been from ear to ear. She would have told her brother that she was off the market, that her heart was Raphael's and his was hers.

What a difference a road trip could make.

She nodded her head and reluctantly whispered back, "Just mates."

"Good. Hey, mate…" He dug into his pocket, pulled out a couple of notes and handed them to Raphael. "You wouldn't mind going to the bar and getting a round, would you?"

Raphael said of course he wouldn't mind, but refused the money saying this one was on him.

He was polite and sophisticated and perfect. He asked them all what they wanted, told Maggie he'd find her something with bubbles in it, then disappeared around the corner.

Would he even bother coming back?

Eddie rejoined them and gave his brother a discreet nod. Not so subtle that she didn't catch it. And, even though she felt her guts launch into Kid Sister Attack Mode, there was a comforting familiarity about it. They all knew their roles. They all played their parts. It was an upside to coming home that she hadn't really considered before. Even if it *did* most likely mean she'd be back in her pinafore and acting the spinster sister and housekeeper until she was an old, shriveled, apple-faced lady. Wrinkled. Hunch-backed, no doubt. Miserable. Alone.

"Cheer up, Dags. It's your party!"

Eddie tried to tickle her and she batted at his hands, reluctantly succumbing to the giggles until he stopped.

"What are you boys cooking up? You haven't got Dad jumping out of a birthday cake or anything, have you?"

Nate shook his head and laughed. "Nah. But I wish we had thought of that." He crossed his arms, swayed back on his heels and gave her a cheeky grin. "I think you're going to like what we've got planned for you. It's one of our best ideas *ever*."

She gave him a wary look. "You mean like slingshotting our father across a vacant lot? Yes. What a terrific idea *that* was. Making us orphans on my birthday."

"Easy, there, little bear cub." Nate gave her shoulder a gentle rub. "Your brothers are looking out for you as you launch into womanhood."

"What, precisely, do you think I have been in these last ten years?"

They laughed. "Mags! Your twenties are just a warm-up for the big stuff. Trust us."

"Not ruddy likely," she grumbled, but they told her to stay put, wait for her drink and they'd come and get her in a few minutes.

She peeked round the corner and saw Raphael, waiting politely for his turn at the bar. Looking completely gorgeous. Of course.

She dug around in her handbag for some lip gloss. Might as well at least remind him of what he was missing.

Her fingers made contact with some paper.

The envelope.

Her heart cinched tight.

Sinking into a nearby chair, she decided to take advantage of the few minutes she had alone and read the note her mother had written to her all those years ago.

The back of her throat grew scratchy at the sight of the handwriting. When she lifted the letter to her nose to smell it hot tears fell in splatters on her skirt.

Forcing herself to take a deep breath and focus, she opened the letter and read.

My darling Maggie-moo,
By the time you get this letter I will have been unable to say goodbye in person. Don't let a single solitary second pass with you thinking I didn't love you with every cell in my body. You are my beautiful green-eyed, red-haired dream come true, and it was my mission in life to help you reach your goals. Or at least give you a nudge in the right direction.

Dry your eyes, love. I know it was a self-ish decision not to tell you, but as well as being a dreamer you're also a realist. If you'd known... Well, it was time for your brothers to help out around the house a bit, and for

ANNIE O'NEIL

261

you to go out there and see the world. A bit of it, at least. The bit that I hoped would inspire you the most.

Your letters were like a window to Paris. Through you I was able to go to the Louvre. Have ice-cream by the Seine. Climb the Eiffel Tower. Especially the Eiffel Tower! I felt as if I was right there beside you. The icing on my cake.

Your father once even made us crêpes based on the recipe you sent. They were awful. But he tried. And that's what I am going to ask you to do.

Please try and let those moments—the "icing" moments—be your lasting memories of our time together. An adventure. And never let anything stand in the way of following your beautiful heart. Wherever it wants to take you, near or far, your family will always be with you, no matter how many kilometers lie between you.

I love you so very much, my little Maggiemoo.

Always think of me as being with you, in your heart, for you will always live in mine.

Don't let your brothers boss you around too

much. They're protective. They love you, even if they lack the ability to buy socks. Keeping you near to them is the only way they know how to keep you safe. But I know you're strong. You'll do just fine on your own.

Bisous, *my darling.*
Love, Mum

Maggie's hands dropped to her lap and she looked up to the ceiling, physically opening herself up to the waves of emotion hitting her.

Bittersweet relief at having the letter, seeing her mother's writing again, being able to cherish her scent.

This letter was the link—the farewell she'd never had.

Most of all she felt love—unconditional love—for her brothers. Sure, they lacked finesse, but they tried. Their campaign to get her to move home had never abated. Not once…until now.

That thought unleashed sorrow. All the frustration and sadness that had gone with the initial loss. Dreams unfulfilled, ambitions unrealized. Had she lost or gained more in the years following her mother's death?

It was something she'd never know.

She looked up, sensing someone approaching. "Maggie, are you all right?"

Raphael quickly slid the tray of drinks onto a nearby table, tugged a small pile of serviettes from the tray and sat beside her, his hand halfway to wiping away her tears when she stopped him.

He was an unrealized dream. She needed to take this letter as a sign that it was time to move on. Some dreams came true—some didn't.

Her brothers appeared at the end of the corridor, bursting with excitement.

She grabbed the serviettes and scrubbed them across her face, almost relishing the scratchy pain that accompanied them. It was a marked contrast to Raphael's soft handkerchief and the love she had thought she had felt.

Well, she wouldn't rely on him anymore. Or on his love. It was her birthday, and she was going to ruddy well enjoy herself. She had her brothers here. *Family*—who, despite everything, had been there for her all along.

"C'mon." She spoke in a low voice so her approaching brothers couldn't hear. "They've gone to a lot of effort. We should at least try to look happy."

* * *

Against his better judgment, Raphael picked up the tray of drinks and pasted on what he hoped passed as a smile.

When Maggie's brothers led them down the corridor and flung open the double doors of a private lounge any hint of happiness dropped from his lips.

In front of him was a huge banner.

Broken Hill Bachelors Got Talent! Who Will Win Our Maggie's Heart?

Her brothers kept looking at the banner, at the pre-lit stage area, and back to Maggie for signs of delight.

She laughed. Punched them in the arm. Then threw Raphael a look that said, *It could've been you*, grabbed her glass of Aussie fizz from his tray and followed her brothers to the throne-like chair they had set up in front of the stage.

What followed was the most painful hour of Raphael's life.

And not just because of the ample talents of the men of Broken Hill.

The Maggie who had opened herself up to him

less than twenty-four hours earlier had all but disappeared.

Whether she was the real one or the one protecting herself from the world's most idiotic Frenchman was tough to tell at this point. He'd lost his perspective.

The one thing he *was* certain of, he decided, between a live chainsaw juggling act and a fairly impressive bit of "condiment art", inspiration courtesy of legendary local artist Pro Hart, was that until he went home and made peace with his own "family" he would never settle. Never be able to offer Maggie everything she so richly deserved.

"Mate!" Nate appeared beside him, tickled pink with the evening's showcase. "Isn't this brilliant? I don't think I've ever seen Maggie have more fun."

Together they looked across at her. She was accepting a vividly decorated rain stick from a suitor who had just performed a rain dance in the hopes of "growing a life together" with Maggie.

She looked completely delighted. If not a little unconvinced.

"We should've asked you, but as Mags said you were just mates we didn't bother. Do you want to go up and do a jig or something? You're looking a little bit as if the green-eyed monster has come to life inside of you." Nate's voice was genuinely concerned and then his eyes widened. "Wait a minute. You're not in *love* with her or anything, are you?"

Raphael just stared at him. Was he that transparent? Luckily Nate wasn't waiting for an answer.

"It's unrequited love, isn't it? Poor bloke. You flew all the way Down Under to get our Mags, only to have her turn you down?"

Again he didn't wait for a response, just blew out a low, *Sorry, pal* whistle and shook his head.

"Rough. She's a bit of a treasure, though. Worth fighting for. You *sure* you don't have a little tune or something you could sing *a capella*? Dad plays the accordion if you need a bit of back-up."

Maggie *was* worth fighting for. But a song wouldn't cover what he needed to do to win her heart.

At the very least, he knew she would be surrounded by people who loved her if he didn't get the answers he was hoping for in Paris.

"I think Maggie looks very happy here."

Nate looked across at his sister. Her green eyes

were glistening, her hair lit by the bright stage lights as yet another suitor pulled her up onto the stage only to perform a traditional Maypole jig around her—Maggie as the Maypole.

He did want her.

He didn't yet deserve her.

But he was going to do everything in his power to do just that.

There was only one way to be worthy of the love she so openly gave him.

Go back to Paris and prove he was the man she had once believed him to be.

Though she was doing her best to look entertained by the dance, Maggie's eyes kept darting towards the dark-haired, blue-eyed man who, despite everything, still drew her like a magnet.

Halfway through the courtship dance that felt more like an endurance contest she saw Raphael whisper something to her brother, then get up and leave.

Her mouth went dry as tingles of fear whispered across her skin.

History was repeating itself.

Why did the people she loved most in life refuse to say goodbye to her face to face?

The thought didn't settle properly.

Her mother had done her best. The letter had been there. It had just… Maybe it had been waiting for the perfect time to surface—to serve as a reminder of the girl she had once been. The woman she had hoped to become.

Raphael stopped at the doorway and turned to look back at her. Every cell in her body ached to run after him, to demand an explanation, to ask why her love wasn't enough. Why *she* wasn't enough.

Steadfastly, she held her ground. She had her mother's faith living in her heart again. She had the knowledge that at least one person in her life had believed she was strong enough to make a go of things alone, to pursue her dreams—at least some of them—until she achieved them.

Medical school wasn't out of the question.

Nor was international travel.

It simply wouldn't be with Raphael.

Defiance and strength replaced fear. She didn't need anyone by her side to confront the future. She just needed to believe in herself.

She was thirty, single, and ready to dream again.

She forced a smile back to her lips as Darren

O'Toole and his steel-toed work boots continued circling around her in a proud display of peacocking. Pounding. Thumping. Clomping round her like an elephant aspiring to be a ballerina. Okay, perhaps her future wouldn't be linked to Darren O'Toole. But there'd be someone out there.

One day.

She looked toward the back of the room. Her eyes connected with Raphael's like an electric shock. There was fire in his gaze. But it was impossible to tell if the flames burnt for *her*.

When he turned and walked away she knew she had her answer.

She'd be facing the future on her own.

CHAPTER ELEVEN

RAPHAEL HAD STOOD in front of this door so many times and never once hesitated. Not like this.

He blew on his hands, chiding himself for not remembering how cold it would be in Paris. Chiding himself for even caring. There was so much more at stake than chafed skin if he didn't take this chance.

A family.

A future.

A heart that would never break again.

He gave the door a sound knock.

When it opened he was face to face with Jean-Luc.

His friend's eyes widened with disbelief as he took a half-step back…then opened his arms and pulled Raphael into a tight embrace…

An hour later, Raphael's only regret was not having come sooner.

Jean-Luc had apologized for flinging blame in

Raphael's direction. He'd been angry with the world. Now he knew, no matter how painful, that his daughter's death had been simply an awful truth he'd had to absorb and live with. Whether Raphael had stayed or left, the end result would very likely have been the same. He saw now that Raphael had been put into an impossible scenario and he no longer felt it necessary to blame anyone.

It had been no one's fault.

Just a cruel turn of events.

"I should have stayed." Raphael shook his head at his own folly. "Stayed with Amalie. Stayed with you. Given you a human punching bag. I just felt so responsible. When your parents said I had to give it time, give you some space—"

"They said that?" Jean-Luc cut in. "Give me some *space*?" He laughed drily. "You took that a bit literally, didn't you? Africa? Australia? You couldn't get much further than that."

"They aren't yet sending commercial passengers to the moon," Raphael riposted, grateful to be engaging once again in the banter that had once fuelled their friendship. "No free clinics to volunteer at in outer space. Yet."

Jean-Luc laughed again. "Well, perhaps they were right. Perhaps we both needed some space, eh, my friend?"

Raphael nodded. He knew now that living as he had been—in the eye of the storm—had been painful and scarring. Now that it had passed he thanked the heavens above for showing him how strong his friendship with Jean-Luc truly was.

"Hang on a minute," Jean-Luc said, slipping the pair of coffee cups off the table and setting them beside the sink. "Would you be able to stay for supper? There is some extra news you should know, but I would like Marianne to be here when I share it."

"*Bien sûr.* I would be delighted."

"Excellent." Jean-Luc crossed to him and gave him a solid hug. "My parents would love to catch up as well. Shall I call them? Make it a proper family meal?"

Emotion caught at Raphael's throat.

A proper family meal.

There was only one person who would be missing—one person who would make the evening perfect.

Twenty-four hours earlier...

"Wait. You *what*?" Maggie stared at her brothers in disbelief.

"We banded together and bought you a ticket to Paris." Billy pressed it into her hand. "Go on. Get out of here."

"I don't understand."

Eddie fuzzed his lips. "C'mon, Dags. Anyone could see that the Broken Hill bachelor brigade didn't hold a single iota of interest for you. You only had eyes for one man in that room, and he was *not* a Broken Hill man."

Maggie laughed at her brother's affronted tone.

"You can't help who you love." Her shoulders hunched up round her ears and she sheepishly scanned them all.

"Love?" Her father gave a pointed look at the wall clock, distractedly scratching a curious Monster behind the ears. "If you don't begin to get a move-on you're going to miss the connecting flight. If I have to get the chief of police to put you in the back of a van to get you there on time, I will."

Tears sprang to her eyes for the millionth time that day. Well, they'd hardly been dry since she'd

274 REUNITED WITH HER PARISIAN SURGEON

insisted on going back home with her brothers after Darren O'Toole had finally finished dancing.

She'd made a mistake. She'd let pride stand in the way of her heart and that was the last lesson she was meant to have learnt from her mother's letter.

Her mother had told her to follow her heart. Not her cerebral hemispheres. Or her hurt feelings.

She loved Raphael, and when he'd got up to leave—

Her thoughts froze. Before he'd left he'd spoken to Nate.

She fixed her brother with her sternest gaze.

"What was it Raphael said to you before he left?"

Nate scuffed his work boots along the ground. "Aw, it was nothing, Dags. Just go get your plane, wouldja?"

"Nathaniel Louis! Your mother did *not* raise you to obfuscate."

"Margaret Louis," her brother countered solidly, "your mother raised you to follow your dreams, and it might have taken us a while to figure it out, but we're pretty bloody sure they're not here in Broken Hill."

He grabbed her keys from the kitchen counter and put them in her hand, then pointed to the carport.

"Now, go out there and get your man. Or become a surgeon. Or both. Otherwise the lot of us are going to have to gaffer tape you up, put you in the boot and get you on the plane ourselves."

Hands on hips, ready to give back as good as she'd got, she suddenly burst into laughter.

She had the *best* family.

She opened her arms wide and pulled them all into a group hug, in which *she* ended up getting squished. Amidst the sprawl of arms and chests and poorly shaved chins she finally managed to elbow enough room for herself to shout, "I love you lot!"

"We love you too, Margaret," her father said, opening a pathway for her to get to her car. "Now, go make us proud and make some dreams come true. And if they don't go the way you thought they would, we'll be right here waiting for you. Monster included. With enough laundry to keep you busy until you're ready to joust again."

Keep on trying.

That should be her family's motto.

And today she was emblazoning that motto straight onto her heart.

"Puis-je...?"
Maggie didn't even have to look up to recognize the man asking if it was all right to sit on the patch of grass next to her.

Her entire nervous system knew his voice.

Her memory banks were covered in images of the two of them in this exact spot.

It was next to her favorite bench. Which was situated at her favorite angle to tip her head back and...

She watched as his legs bent at the knee, then his waist came into view, and his long fingers, pressing into the grass alongside her.

"How did you know I was here?"

Maggie could barely look up, her heart was thumping so rapidly. When she did, the Raphael she'd seen that night in the motel met her eyes. Blue irises, pure as the uncharacteristically clear spring sky. Lips parted in a half-smile that all but invited her to jump into his arms and kiss him.

He pulled his phone from his pocket and shook it. "Your brothers. I believe you just sent them a picture message of yourself at the Eiffel Tower."

Maggie frowned. She had, but… "How did they know—?" She stopped. "Is *that* what you told Nate. You gave him your phone number?"

"Non." He looked a bit confused himself before crossing his legs and sitting beside her on the ground. "I said if you hadn't heard from me in three days to hold another talent show. And another. Until you found someone who deserved you."

"Why would you have said that?" The note of defensiveness she'd hoped to keep from her voice leapt to the fore.

"Because I wasn't sure I would ever have anything to offer you."

"What? I don't want things. I want *you*!"

The words were out before she stood any chance of preserving her dignity. She stood up and gave the ground beneath her a stomp, reminding herself she hadn't flown halfway round the world to make idle chitchat.

Raphael stood up and met her gaze straight on.

"Good," he said, a glint of anticipation lighting up his eyes.

"Good?" she parroted.

"Oui. Good. But I have two questions before I tell you why."

Maggie tilted her chin to the side and gave him her best suspicious look. The one that said, *If you are messing with me I am turning around and flying back to Australia whilst ensuring every single person on that plane, and perhaps the whole of Australia, knows just how much of a jerk I think you are. Even if you're gorgeous. And I love you.*

"I love you," Raphael said.

"I just said that!"

"What? No, you didn't. You haven't said anything."

"I did. I said I loved you." She pointed to herself. "In my *head*. Which means we're connected. And that means you should stop running away from things, and stop jumping onto planes when people shout or yell. Or when you are forced to watch your girl be the guest of honor at incredibly ridiculous talent shows."

"Maggie." Raphael lifted a finger to her lips. "Will you just listen for a minute so I can explain? A bit of clog hopping is not going to keep me from loving you."

She tried her best not to give his finger a kiss. She was still supposed to be angry. Defiant, even. But she couldn't resist. Not when his touch unleashed a wash of glittery fireworks inside her that would have lit up the Eiffel Tower if it hadn't been broad daylight.

She kissed his finger. "See?" She grinned. "Proof I love you."

"And I wanted to get *you* proof."

"What? Why would you have to—?" She stopped herself. "You've been to see Jean-Luc?"

Raphael nodded. "And, if you would care to join me, you and I are invited to dine with them tonight."

Maggie's heart exploded with relief for him. "That's amazing, Raphael. I am so happy for you. *All* of you."

He nodded, his smile truly lighting up his face. "And, even better, his wife is pregnant. They are expecting twins!"

A wash of pure gold heat warmed her body. "That's incredible news. I'm so happy for them. For you."

"And perhaps for us?"

A tiny part of her wanted to play the coquette. To make him suffer just a tiny bit for all the nail-biting her poor fingers had endured during the long flight over. But he'd been through the wringer these past couple of years. And besides, if she'd learned anything at all in the past forty-eight hours it was that life was too short to dither. She'd flown here to get answers.

"What exactly are you saying?"

"I am saying, or rather I am asking, Margaret Louis, if you would accompany me to dinner with the Couttards as my fiancée. And then, perhaps another time, as my wife?"

"Perhaps?" she yelped. "Perhaps! You mean definitely."

Raphael's smile was unfettered. "Is that a yes?"

"You bet it is."

She could barely speak, she was so happy. And then the questions flooded in.

"Where are we going to live? Do you still want to work on the ambos? Do you hate Australia? Love it? How would you feel if I went to medical school?"

"Right now I have no idea. All I know is wherever I am, I want it to be with you." Raphael pulled her close to him and her hands naturally slipped up and around his neck. "Now, my beautiful Maggie, would you allow me the pleasure of kissing my fiancée?"

"I think that is a most excellent idea."

Maggie rose up on tiptoe and, with a fully open heart, accepted the very first kiss from her future husband.

EPILOGUE

"ARE YOU SURE it looks all right?" Maggie squinted at her reflection and shifted the white lab coat collar to the left.

"You look perfect, Dr. Bouchon. What time is the flight going to leave?"

Maggie glanced at her watch. "Probably in an hour." She laughed, her eyes connecting with Raphael's in the mirror. "I still can't get used to this."

"What? The flying doctor part or the Dr. Bouchon part?" Raphael slipped his hands round his wife's waist and dropped a kiss onto her neck.

"Either." Maggie turned and gave her husband a kiss. A hit of emotion clouded her eyes for a moment. "I wish my mum could see this. I wish she could know I've finally become a doctor."

Raphael smiled at his wife's reflection in the mirror. "She does. Because she's living—"

"In my heart," Maggie finished, knowing full

well that it was true. "I wonder what she would think of our lives now."

"What? Living in Broken Hill and taking our winter holidays in France?"

"Yeah." Maggie giggled. "Part of me thinks she would tell us we're absolutely bonkers…"

She looked out of the window to where her brothers were building a super-sized swing set for their toddlers.

"The other part thinks she might've known this would happen."

"As long as you are happy, *mon amour*. That's all that matters."

She turned around in her husband's arms and embraced him tightly. "I have everything I have ever dreamed of here and now."

"Très bien." He dropped a kiss onto her cheek and took her hand in his. "Shall we make sure your brothers aren't planning to trebuchet our children over to the next-door neighbors?"

"How well you know them." She gave him a wink and, hand in hand, they headed out to be with the rest of their family.

* * * * *

LET'S TALK

Romance

For exclusive extracts, competitions
and special offers, find us online:

f facebook.com/millsandboon

⊙ @millsandboonuk

🐦 @millsandboon

Or get in touch on 0844 844 1351*

For all the latest titles coming soon,
visit millsandboon.co.uk/nextmonth

*Calls cost 7p per minute plus your phone company's price per
minute access charge

Want even more
ROMANCE?

Join our bookclub today!

**Visit millsandbook.co.uk/Bookclub
and save on brand new books.**

MILLS & BOON